"I love you, Catherine. You've become my whole life."

David took a deep breath. "Something has come up to do with my work, and you need to be told about it."

He felt her eyes on him. "Are you talking about the institute?"

"Yes. As you know, we compile data on identical twins. But there's another aspect to this. We also put out ads to attract people who think they *might* be twins."

"What do you mean, think?" she asked.

"Some people write or phone the institute telling us they've had experiences that lead them to believe they've got a twin somewhere, even though there's no real proof. Twice so far, we've been the catalyst to bring separated twins together."

"That's extraordinary!"

"But," he said, "consider for a moment how someone might feel if he or she had no knowledge of being a twin and was then confronted by this long-lost sibling."

"It would be such a shock, I can't even imagine it. Of course, my brother Jack would probably love it, since he's been wanting to find his birth parents for quite a while now." She stopped suddenly. "Are you saying Jack has an identical twin who's been looking for him?"

"I wish I could say yes to your question."

It took a minute for David's words to sink in. "*I'm* the one with the twin, aren't I?"

Dear Reader,

I don't know about you, but the phenomenon of identical twins has always fascinated me. In fact, my interest grew to the point that I wrote a novel, *The Wrong Twin*, several years ago for Harlequin Superromance.

That particular story explored the world of identical twin sisters who were raised together, adored each other and shared everything, even their love for the same man. In that novel I focused on the special *psychic* bond between identical twins.

In my latest book, *The Unknown Sister*, I've written a tale of identical twin sisters who were separated at birth. They come from entirely different backgrounds and circumstances and would never have met if they hadn't happened to fall in love with the same man. In this novel, I've explored the *psychological* aspects of their extraordinary situation.

I hope you'll find their story as riveting and intriguing as I did in writing it.

Rebecca Winters

Books by Rebecca Winters

HARLEQUIN SUPERROMANCE

THE UNKNOWN
SISTER
Rebecca
Winters

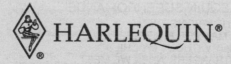

HARLEQUIN®

TORONTO • NEW YORK • LONDON
AMSTERDAM • PARIS • SYDNEY • HAMBURG
STOCKHOLM • ATHENS • TOKYO • MILAN • MADRID
PRAGUE • WARSAW • BUDAPEST • AUCKLAND

ISBN 0-373-70916-1

THE UNKNOWN SISTER

Copyright © 2000 by Rebecca Winters.

To Michael,
whose brilliant insights
make this world a better place for all.

Bless you.

CHAPTER ONE

"STEADY, JACK! The red Ford Taurus is trying to box you in. Don't let him get on your left. Easy. Be careful. Keep going! That's it! Hold on!"

Catherine Casey's breath caught as her brother's rebuilt purple Chev with the yellow sunbursts flew around the turn at the Portland stock car racetrack. "Keep holding. Don't give up your spot now. Keep holding. Yes!" she cried in excitement when he moved ahead.

Too bad his girlfriend, Melanie, had to be out of town for a family reunion this weekend. Otherwise, she would've been here, too. Catherine suspected this girl was the one for Jack. Of course, only time would tell.

What a shame the rest of the family couldn't have come to see his performance, either, especially their two older married brothers, Brody and Mark. Today everybody who normally supported him had prior commitments they couldn't get out of. So did Catherine, but she'd promised to watch a portion of the race.

She was two years older than her intense, sandy-haired brother. Jack had turned twenty-five last month. She felt especially close to him, probably because he'd been adopted soon after her and they'd been raised like twins.

Jack's fascination with racing had begun when he was thirteen. Their parents had taken him on a business trip to Ohio with them, and they'd stopped at the Eldon Speedway in Rossberg; ever since then, he'd wanted to be a race car driver. Catherine still remembered how he'd come running into the house after their return home, sporting a World 100 T-shirt.

Racing was in his blood, the way architecture was in hers. Over the last twelve years he'd earned his master mechanic's degree and had gone into business with his best friend, Phil. They leased a garage from her dad and had equipped it to run their own body shop. During the day, Jack and Phil, plus their hired crew, worked on other people's cars to earn their living. After hours, Jack was building his own race car and was making a name for himself locally. The whole family was proud of his achievements.

His dream was to win the Save Mart/Kragen 350 NASCAR Winston Cup at the Sears Point speedway in California. Such a victory would be a stepping-stone to even bigger wins. But he needed close to seven million dollars to build a new car and put together a salaried team.

Their dad had contributed half the money toward his goal. The rest needed to come from other members of the family, friends, sponsors and Jack's earnings from various races. A first place today would net him ten thousand dollars. He had to win!

With the aid of her binoculars, Catherine looked for the number of the red car trying to edge him out of the race. Pausing for a moment, she scanned the program. Number twenty-four was being driven by Mitch Britton, another contender from Portland. The name sounded familiar. According to the stats, he had almost as many racing points as Jack, and an equal number of wins.

While she studied the list of drivers, a gust of cold wind blew the paper right out of her hand. In dismay she watched it dance over the heads of the crowd of spectators filling the bleachers. There was no way she could run after it.

She shivered as another gust of wind sent programs flying. One glance at the overcast sky told her it would rain any minute. A good thing she'd worn warm clothes to the track. She fastened the top two wooden buttons of her heavy wool sweater before lifting the binoculars to her eyes once more.

Jack still had a half hour's worth of laps to go before the black-and-white checkered flags signaled the end of the race. She wished she could stay to the finish, but an important client had requested a conference concerning his new rental premises, one she'd had to cancel last week due to a bad cold. She couldn't possibly disappoint him a second time.

At least she had the satisfaction of knowing that Jack had seen her in the stands when he'd made his last pit stop. She put her binoculars in her tote bag, then started making her way to the end of the row.

"Excuse me." She tried not to step on people's

toes. "Forgive me," she murmured after running into a hard, trousered leg.

The man stood up to allow her to reach the stairs. She lifted her head, thanking him with a smile. But her apology did nothing to erase the barest trace of revulsion in those midnight-blue eyes staring at her from beneath dark brows and hair.

"I think maybe it's time you and I had a little talk, Shannon."

She blinked. Even with the noise from the cars roaring around the track, she was quite sure he'd called her Shannon.

"I'm afraid you have me mixed up with someone else. Sorry again for disturbing you."

Without wasting another second, she rushed down the stairs toward the exit. Rain had started to fall. If she made a dash to her car, she might not get completely soaked before she could slide behind the wheel of the restored green MG she'd bought several years earlier.

She loved the sound of the motor, the way the little car could dart in and out of traffic. But as she left the parking area with her windshield wipers going, her thoughts weren't on her car.

Whoever Shannon was, Catherine felt sorry for the woman. If a man as masculine and attractive as that well-dressed stranger had ever looked at Catherine with such a lack of pleasure, she would have been shattered.

Vaguely troubled by the encounter, she frowned. At some time in the past she'd heard that everyone on earth had a double, but she'd never given any thought to it until now. She'd certainly never taken it seriously.

To her recollection, no one had mistaken her for anyone else before.

How odd to think another woman walking around Portland—someone apparently called Shannon—resembled Catherine enough, that this man would address her by Shannon's name. The deep vibrancy of his voice still resonated inside her.

She waited for a light to change, then merged with the afternoon traffic headed into the downtown area.

What really puzzled her was the fact that he'd waited until he'd looked into her eyes before calling her Shannon. The man was ready for some kind of confrontation.

Sometimes Catherine had seen a superficial resemblance to a friend or acquaintance in a stranger. But the second she got closer or caught a glance of his or her face, she realized her mistake before approaching that person.

That wasn't the case today. He'd sounded as if he was absolutely certain, as if there could be no mistake.

Maybe the whole thing was upsetting her because the last time she'd met a man who attracted her so strongly, she'd been a naive twenty-year-old junior in undergraduate school. She'd fallen for a teaching assistant who'd pretended to be in love with her in order to pass off her work as his own.

The painful lesson had taught her not to trust men

in general, good-looking ones in particular. Except for the men in her own family, of course.

Perhaps she found herself thinking about the stranger more than she normally would have because he'd mistaken her for someone else and she couldn't help being intrigued.

Whatever the explanation, she had to acknowledge that chemistry probably had more to do with the reason she'd felt disturbed by the incident. There was no denying he was one of the most attractive men she'd ever met.

She stepped on the gas. Five minutes later, the security guard waved to her as she drove into the underground car park of Casey & Associates, the architectural firm where she worked with her father.

Forget the stranger, Catherine. You've got too much to do!

WHILE THE RAIN beat down on his black Mercedes, David Britton sat behind the wheel in a total stupor. Everyone else was watching the race. His brother, Mitch, might even be winning it right now, but David's mind was on the woman who'd tripped over his leg in the bleachers a few minutes ago.

When he'd spotted Shannon sitting farther down the bench at the start of the race, his instinct had been to leave the speedway and avoid her altogether.

But he realized if he did that, he would only be putting off the inevitable. Since he didn't relish the thought of her coming up with a new plan to "accidentally" bump into him, he'd decided to wait until she made her move. Then he'd deliver a few home truths.

Like the fact that they weren't a couple, and she needed to get on with her life.

But it wasn't that simple. Because they had a business relationship…of sorts.

Shannon White had answered one of the thousands of Internet and newspaper ads he'd placed around the country asking for people to participate in a study on identical twins he was conducting at his institute. People who were twins—or believed they'd been separated from their twins at birth and were trying to find them—were invited to respond.

David had created the institute for personal reasons, having lost a younger brother, Mitch's identical twin, to SIDS, a tragedy that had caused untold grief to his mother, who was herself a twin. But he'd grown increasingly interested in the subject and spent more time at the institute now than he did at his stock-trading firm. He'd hired psychologists and funded a laboratory to conduct genetic research on identical twins.

Already the research had proved that the rate of SIDS deaths was higher among identical twins. He'd hoped those facts had comforted his mother, who'd held herself responsible for a death she couldn't have prevented.

David had become so immersed in running the institute, he hadn't made much time for anyone except his widowed mother and Mitch. He'd ended his last relationship with a woman several months ago.

But after his first interview with Shannon, he'd broken his rule about never socializing with a participant and had asked her out to dinner. Between her intelligence and gorgeous blond looks, he found he wanted to know her better.

To his disappointment, however, the evening didn't measure up to his expectations. He couldn't explain exactly why. Nothing had changed since the interview, except that he realized he didn't feel an emotional connection, after all.

Frustrated because the evening had gone flat, he'd hoped to find the elusive spark by kissing her goodnight outside her hotel-room door. She'd shown every sign of wanting more than just talk.

Unfortunately, the chemistry wasn't there.

After thanking her for going out with him, he told her she'd hear from the institute if any data came in suggesting there might be a match. He'd thought she understood he was dismissing the possibility of a romantic involvement.

The next morning, nothing could have surprised him more than to arrive at his office and be told by his secretary that Shannon White was on the line. David assumed she must have forgotten to tell him something relevant to her case. In reality, she'd called to ask if he was free for lunch before she left town.

As tactfully as he could, he told her he had other commitments. He thanked her for the invitation, but was careful not to add that they'd have to get together again some time.

It was bad enough that she continued to phone him over the next few weeks. But he almost lost his patience the Friday she showed up in his office at noon, just as he was leaving to watch one of Mitch's races.

At least he could tell her, with a clear conscience, that he was busy, although he still had to be careful to choose the right words so he wouldn't alienate her. After all, she'd responded to the institute's ad in the hope that her twin sibling, if she really had one, would contact the institute, too. On principle, he needed to treat her as he would any other participant.

But that was the hell of it. He'd done the total opposite. Blinded by her attractiveness, he'd made the mistake of asking her out on a date, of kissing her good-night. Now he was forced to walk the fine line between extending her professional courtesy and ignoring her, and he had no one but himself to blame.

Her presence at the speedway today made him realize she wasn't about to go away. Obviously, during the one and only time they'd gone out together, she'd stored the information he'd told her about Mitch and his passion for race car driving.

When she couldn't get David to ask her out again, she'd decided to make an unexpected appearance at the track, knowing he couldn't very well tell her he had other plans for the afternoon.

Aware that the situation had escalated into something potentially ugly, he'd decided to have it out with her, race or no race, even if it meant offending her in the process. There was just one problem with that scenario.

The woman who'd apologized for bumping into him wasn't Shannon.

The shock had made him slow on the uptake. Not until she'd disappeared from the stands did he realize he'd just met Shannon's missing twin. A woman, not a man.

The unknown sister.

David couldn't begin to estimate the odds of this chance occurrence, not when Shannon wasn't even positive her adoptive mother had been lucid at the time of her deathbed confession.

But *he* was positive.

The two sisters had identical faces and figures. The same feather-cut blond hair, gray eyes and curving mouths.

Yet when she'd looked at him just now, telling him he must have mistaken her for someone else, the warmth of her smile seemed to permeate his bones. Her voice, her expression, her eyes—they all divulged a world of difference between her and Shannon.

Then, before he'd had time to react, she'd vanished in the rain, leaving him breathless with myriad impressions.

Her eyes.

They'd been so alive, they'd recalled swirling storm clouds etched in silver to make them glow.

Everything about her glowed, especially the strands of silvery-gold hair blowing in the wind.

She was like Shannon—and yet she wasn't.

She reminded him of someone who knew a wonderful secret and could hardly contain her excitement. Then she'd run away.

By the time David had recovered enough to go after her, she'd long since left the parking area in a vintage-model green MG. He'd been too far away to make out the numbers on her license plate.

He had no idea who she was. He didn't have a name. But the rush of adrenaline doing crazy things to his heart told him he had to find her. Otherwise, he felt with an odd certainty, nothing in his life would ever make sense again.

Even while he plotted how to go about tracing her, he heard a voice inside his head.

What about Shannon? When do you plan to tell her the news?

As he started the engine and drove out of the parking lot, his hands tightened on the steering wheel.

He didn't want to think about that question right now, let alone consider answering it.

There was something he had to do first, something he had to find out.

MELANIE HAD GIVEN Catherine explicit instructions to visit Jack after her client consultation. He usually experienced a sense of letdown, a feeling of being at loose ends whenever he finished a race, and Melanie tried to spend a few hours with him directly afterward.

Catherine slipped in the side door of the mechanic's garage attached to the garage of the Casey family home. It looked like she'd arrived just in time. The purple Chev had already been parked in its spot, and Jack was revving his restored 911 Porsche, ready to take off somewhere.

"Congratulations, Jack! Sorry I had to leave the race early today, but Mom and Dad told me the wonderful news. You're now ten thousand dollars closer to your goal!"

"Thanks, CC." As long as she could remember, Jack had called her by her initials. She noticed his brown eyes didn't reflect his usual excitement.

"Hey—what's wrong?"

He hunched his shoulders. "I guess you didn't hear about the crash before the end of the race. Bernie Phelp's car went out of control and he took two other cars with him. They're all in the hospital."

Her expression sobered. "That's awful. Did you know the other drivers who were injured?"

"Not personally, but one of them—Mitch Britton—might have come in first if he hadn't been involved in the accident."

Racing was a dangerous sport. Accidents happened all the time, but Catherine tried hard not to think about that. If Jack was ever seriously injured, she couldn't imagine how she'd deal with it—let alone losing her brother. Brody had been in a near-fatal small plane crash a few years earlier. The family didn't need to go through that kind of emotionally wrenching experience again.

"He was driving the red Taurus that gave you a run for your money, wasn't he?"

"That's right." Jack nodded. "He's good, CC. Let's hope they're going to be okay. I never feel like it's a fair race when anyone ends up hurt."

"I don't blame you. Do you know which hospital they were taken to?"

"Yeah. Sacred Heart. I'm headed there right now."

"I'd be happy to go with you if you want some company."

"You don't have a date tonight?"

"No. At the moment my love life is boring."

"Get in, then."

Catherine ran around to the passenger side and slipped inside. He pressed the remote for the garage door. The instant it opened, they shot down the paved drive leading away from the house. Whenever she got the chance, which wasn't very often since Melanie had entered the picture, she enjoyed driving with her brother. He was an expert who knew when to let it rip and when to slow down.

"Oh...I adore it out here so close to the woods. Smell the air tonight. Don't you love it after it's rained?"

"Why don't you move back home? We all miss you."

"I miss all of you, too, but my condo in town is

two minutes from work and I'm getting busier all the time.''

"You've got Dad's flair for design. That's why. One day the sign on the building is going to read Casey, Casey and Associates.''

"Don't I wish!'' She turned to him. "Funny, isn't it?''

"What do you mean?''

"We're all adopted, so I didn't inherit his architectural talent.''

"Maybe camping out on steel girders with him as soon as you could toddle meant you inherited it by osmosis.''

She laughed lightly. "You think? I've often wondered where *you* got the desire to race cars.''

"Not from Mom and Dad, that's for sure.''

"No.'' She laughed again.

"Now, if I could ever find my birth parents, maybe I'd have the answer.''

Catherine rolled her eyes. "You still feel a need to know who they are?''

"Yup. It's got nothing to do with Mom and Dad. You know that. But I can't stop wondering about the blood running through my veins.''

"It's blue, like everyone else's.''

"Very funny. Don't you ever wonder if you're part Scot or English, maybe, or Swedish? I want to know about my roots. Melanie can trace both sides of her family back at least six generations. I'd love to be able to do that.'' He glanced at her. "I've never figured out why you're not driven by the same curiosity."

"Of course I'm curious. But as I've told you before, I can't imagine having parents as great as Mom and Dad. Maybe I'm afraid to look for my birth parents in case they come as too great a disappointment. Perhaps that's the biggest difference between you and me. You're willing to take huge risks."

"That all depends."

"What are you talking about?"

"Want to know a secret?"

"I thought I knew most of yours."

"Not this one. Are you ready?" When she nodded, he said, "I don't like heights."

"You're joking!"

"Nope."

"But you don't mind planes."

"That's different."

She stared at him, remembering the times he'd found an excuse not to walk around an unfinished building with her or their dad.

"So that's the reas—"

"Yup."

"I had no idea. You seem so fearless in every other way."

"To me you're the fearless one, stepping out on those girders."

"Maybe your birth father's a coal miner."

He flashed her a quick smile. "Or serving in the military on a sub."

"The possibilities are endless, aren't they?" she mused.

"Yeah. I might even have brothers and sisters."

"You do!" she blurted. "You've got Mark and Brody, and you've definitely got me!"

"So I do, and I wouldn't change any one of you for all the racing cups in existence."

"Well, that's nice to hear," she said. "But you lose a certain amount of credibility when you exaggerate like that, you know."

He laughed as he performed some breathtaking maneuvers in his Porsche.

Too bad the freeway leading to the hospital in downtown Portland was always crowded. Considering the mood she was in, she would just as soon Jack let the car fly. She craved the mindless exhilaration of speed, since she still felt a little disoriented, a little on edge. After all, it wasn't every day she met a handsome stranger like the man at the track. Just remembering him made her heart leap frantically.

What were the chances of bumping into him again? Ten zillion to one?

DAVID STOOD as the ER physician entered the cubicle. "I finally got the X rays back. Despite your accident, there's no concussion and no broken bones. You're free to go," he said to Mitch. "I've written a prescription for a painkiller. You can fill it at the pharmacy. It's located in the next wing over."

"I know where it is. Thanks, Doc. Before you leave, how are the other guys who were brought in?"

"One's already been released. The other suffered a broken foot. He'll be ready to go home as soon as his cast is on."

"That's good news."

"All in all, you guys were lucky. Take it easy for a while, okay? Give your body a rest."

Mitch nodded.

As soon as the doctor had gone, David helped his brother put on a buttoned shirt he'd brought from home. No way could Mitch lift his arms over his head.

"Thank God you're going to walk out of here with only a bad headache and a couple of bruised ribs." He was thinking of their mother as he said it.

"Yeah. I thought for sure something got smashed this time." With David's help he pulled on his jeans. "We don't need to stop by the pharmacy. I've got painkillers left over from my last accident."

"I assumed as much. I'll bring the car around to the entrance. Why don't you call Mother and tell her I'm driving you back to your apartment? If she hears your voice, it'll calm her down." David saw him hesitate. "Just do it, Mitch."

David had no problem with his brother's latest craze. In fact he'd backed him in his race car driving. But when it came to their mother, who'd been overprotective of Mitch since the death of the other twin, Mitch preferred to have his older brother fight his battles.

It was understandable. Their mother lived alone, and she was still grieving for their father, who'd died of a heart attack four years earlier.

Mitch felt guilty enough for moving out of the house a year ago, let alone for pursuing several high-risk hobbies that went against her wishes. Still, David knew his brother had reached his limit—he couldn't deal with her anxiety any longer. David did what he could to run interference, but there were times, like now, when Mitch needed to deal with their mother himself.

When David pulled up in front of the sliding glass doors of the emergency room a few minutes later, Mitch emerged with a brooding expression on his face. Even if the phone conversation hadn't gone well, David was pleased Mitch had called their mother. As long as there was communication, there was hope.

Once he'd climbed into the passenger seat and they were on their way, David turned to him. ''You hungry?''

''No. When I get home, I'll have a beer. That's the only thing that sounds good to me right now.''

''I'll join you,'' David said. ''Look, Mitch, I'm sorry I wasn't there when the accident happened. Something unexpected came up, and I had to leave the bleachers. I didn't learn about Phelp's car catching fire until I got home. I played back the messages on my answering machine and heard mother's version of things.''

"Hey, that's okay.'' Mitch shrugged, then winced—the movement had obviously hurt his ribs. "I'm always surprised you get to as many races as you do,'' he continued. "There wasn't anything you could have done about it, anyway.''

"That's true. Accidents are part of the game. But Mother lives in constant fear because she sees you as risking your life over and over for no reason. Have you ever thought of going to counseling to learn how to help her understand you better?''

"You mean talking to some quack?''

"No. I mean seeing a really good psychiatrist. My friend Allen used to go to one after his wife was suddenly killed. Those visits helped him get through that really rough period. Now he's married again and happy.'' David glanced at his brother. "I'd go with you, Mitch. Maybe a professional could teach us how to get through to Mother so her fears won't overwhelm her so much. Think about it.''

After a long silence, Mitch said, "You'd come, too?''

"That's right. You're going to be in a lot more races down the road. I can't say I'm looking forward to dealing with more of your guilt and her paranoia.''

"No kidding,'' he muttered. "Okay. If Allen vouches for him, go ahead and make an appointment. It would be nice to get Mother off my back, once and for all.''

"I'll get in touch with Dr. Morton, then." David relaxed against the back of the seat.

One subject down, one to go.

"If that accident hadn't happened today, you still would've won the race, you know."

"I doubt it. Jack Casey's hot, and getting hotter."

"I grant you he's good, but what's a little healthy competition? You're better."

Mitch flashed him a grin. "So, big brother, tell me what was more important than watching the rest of my race today. Did some gorgeous groupie see you in the stands and decide to proposition you instead of one of the drivers?"

"You got the gorgeous part right. But she was no groupie. If anyone was about to do the propositioning, you're looking at him."

Mitch let out a groan because he'd straightened in his seat too fast. "You're putting me on."

"Not about this. The problem is, she ran off before I could get an address or a phone number."

He blinked. "What's her name?"

"I have no idea. She was already gone by the time I reached the parking lot."

"Then how are you going to find her?"

"That's the problem I wanted to talk to you about. She did leave one clue. Maybe you can help me."

David felt his brother's speculative gaze.

"Are you telling me you're interested in some woman you saw in the stands? A woman who was more exciting than my race?"

A smile lifted a corner of David's mouth. "I realize that's a little hard for you to imagine."

"Not with some guys, it isn't. But we're talking about you."

"You thought I was immune to good-looking women?" he mocked.

"Hell, no. But I never knew you to react like this to a perfect stranger before."

With that comment, David sobered. "That's the whole point, Mitch. She wasn't a stranger. At least, I didn't think she was at the time."

Mitch shook his head. "You know something, David? Your brains must be scrambled or something. If I weren't in major pain right now, I'd say *you* were the one who had the accident today instead of me." He sighed. "Okay, what's the clue and how can I help?"

"I thought you'd never ask. I need you to use all your resources to locate a garage that does work on a restored vintage-model, hunter-green MG."

"That's what this babe was driving?"

He nodded. "I'll make it worth your time."

Mitch eyed him in shock. "You're serious!"

"Dead serious."

"How much are we talking?"

"Find her for me within a week and you'll get a bonus in your paycheck."

"What if I find her in twenty-four hours?"

"Then you can name your price."

"You're on!"

CHAPTER TWO

"EXCUSE ME. I'd like to know the status of the three race car drivers who were brought to Emergency from the Portland speedway this afternoon. Their last names were Phelp, Britton and Clark."

The triage nurse looked up from her charts. "Are you related to one of them?"

"No. I was driving in the same race. I want to know if they're all right."

"Just a minute."

As she walked through a set of swinging doors, Jack confided, "We're not going to learn anything. I probably should have lied."

Catherine shook her head. "I'm sure she'll tell us something. Do you want to watch TV while we wait? There's nobody in reception except a man who's fallen asleep."

"I wouldn't be able to concentrate. But go ahead if you want."

"No. I'll stay with you."

"I hate hospitals."

"I do, too."

Within seconds the nurse came back through the doors. "You're too late. All three have been released. One went home with a cast on his foot. The other two had no serious injuries.''

Jack's face reflected relief. ''That's all I needed to know. Thanks.''

''You're welcome.''

''Let's get out of here,'' he muttered to Catherine.

She waited until they were in the car. ''Now we can celebrate!''

''Is that why you're all dressed up?''

''Yes. Melanie asked me to take you to dinner if you won. She even gave me the money.''

A light entered his eyes. ''She did?''

''Yes. That's why I came over to the house tonight. She knew you'd be feeling sorry for yourself.''

He grinned. ''So where are we going?''

''What do you feel like?''

''Steak.''

''Perfect. There's a new steak restaurant in that warehouse I redesigned last winter.''

''The building all of Portland is talking about. My big sister's triumph. Yeah. Let's go there. I'm starving!''

Catherine enjoyed her brother's company anytime, but she knew the evening would be delightful—just the distraction she needed. Now that Jack was reassured his girlfriend had remembered him, he'd reverted to his usual charming self. Which was a relief, because Catherine had been at a loose end herself since the incident with the stranger.

Every time she thought about the attractive man

at the speedway, excitement surged through her body. The longer she put off going to bed, the better.

Saturday night in downtown Portland meant there were few parking spaces available. Jack drove around the underground parking area for at least ten minutes before finding a spot.

"It's a good thing that didn't take any longer," he murmured as they got out of the car. "I'm about to expire from hunger." Catherine could believe it. Her wiry, five-foot-ten brother required more food than most people, but his intensity affected his metabolism and prevented him from putting on weight. Lucky guy.

After the maitre d' had seated them, a younger man approached. "Hi! I'm Steve, and I'll be your waiter tonight."

He handed Jack a menu, but when Catherine's turn came, he held back. There was an appreciative gleam in his eyes. "I think I know what you want."

Jack gave her a knowing glance.

A smile broke out on her face. At twenty-eight years of age, she found it flattering, if not amusing, to have a college-age guy flirt with her.

"What would that be?"

"Filet mignon with champignons and raspberry sorbet for dessert. Correct?"

"That sounds delicious. Make mine very well done."

The waiter looked perplexed. "Last time you ordered it medium rare."

Last time?

"I beg your pardon?"

His glance darted to Jack before returning to her. "Oh, I get it. Sorry."

"Have you been holding out on me, CC?" Jack gave her a pretended fierce look. "I thought you said you'd never been here before. Now I find out you came with some other guy!"

"But I didn't!"

The waiter gave her a menu. "I must have mistaken you for someone else. Sorry. I'll be back in a minute for your orders."

"Wait!" Catherine called.

"Yes?"

"You really thought I'd been here before?"

He hesitated, his eyes flicking to Jack.

"Please, Steve. This is important."

"Yeah. Maybe two, three weeks ago, I waited on this couple for dinner. It isn't often you see a woman with such beautiful hair and—well, a woman as good-looking as you. You don't happen to have an identical twin sister, do you?"

This was the second time in one day!

She took a deep breath. "The man she was with— was he, by any chance, tall?"

"As a matter of fact, he was."

"Did he have dark brown hair and blue eyes?"

"Yeah." He nodded. "That sounds like him. Strong build, mid-thirties, expensive suit."

It sounded exactly like the stranger!

"Steve—I'm ready to order. I'll have the filet,

well done, plus a baked potato and tossed salad with vinegar and oil dressing.''

Jack said, ''I'll have the same, but make mine medium rare.''

The waiter took their menus. When he was out of earshot, Jack turned to Catherine.

''I thought our new friend Steve was just coming on to you.''

''So did I. At first,'' she added quietly. ''Jack? The strangest thing happened to me at the speedway today.'' Needing to talk about it, she told him the details. ''I didn't know what to make of it until the waiter mistook me for her, too.''

''That's pretty weird, all right. Why didn't you ask the man at the track more questions?''

Warmth filled her cheeks. ''I would have liked to, but it was an awkward moment. He was staring at me with such distaste. Besides, I was late for an important appointment.''

''Too bad you didn't stay long enough to learn the last name of your double. You might have been able to look her up.'' He sat back in his chair. ''Maybe the waiter remembers her name. I'll ask.''

''No! Please don't.''

''Why not?''

''Because it's not important.''

''Maybe not, but you have to admit it's interesting. If there's another woman who looks identical to you living in Portland, I think it would be fun to meet her.''

''I disagree.''

"What are you scared of?"

"I don't know. It's one thing to bear a superficial resemblance to someone else. But to actually pass for another person? I think that's spooky. Like nature made a mistake or something. Let's not talk about it anymore."

"I'm sure Steve was exaggerating."

"You're probably right. Still, after my experience with the stranger today... Promise me you won't say anything to our waiter."

He raised both hands. "All right. I won't."

"Thank you."

After dinner, Steve brought the bill. Catherine took the envelope with Jack's name on it out of her purse. Inside was the money Melanie had given her to pay for their meal.

Jack saw Melanie's writing and removed it from her hands. "It was the thought that counted. I'm taking care of this." He pulled out his credit card and placed it on the tray.

As Steve walked off, Jack smiled mysteriously, folded the envelope and put it in his pocket. "When Melanie gets home, she'll receive her reward."

Catherine reflected on the way her brother's eyes ignited whenever his girlfriend's name came up in conversation. That was the way it should be when someone had fallen in love.

It was hard not to compare his look of happiness to the frigid eyes of the stranger at the speedway. For some reason, the incident refused to leave her mind.

She couldn't figure out why she felt such a strong attraction to him, when the nature of her business meant she worked around a lot of appealing men. The only trouble was, so far none of them had made the same kind of impact.

AFTER FINISHING AN INTERVIEW with a new participant in the twins study, David grabbed his briefcase and left the office on a run. The decision he'd made two years ago—to step down as CEO of the stock-trading company he owned—had been the right one. Since that time, he'd been able to oversee the growth of the institute he'd created.

With Bob Ames successfully managing the trading company that had made David a fortune by his late twenties, he'd been freed to do what he considered his life's work.

It pleased him that the institute's activities had expanded to the point that he needed a larger structure. As soon as he and Mitch were finished with their doctor's appointment, he planned to begin the process of building a new place; in fact, he had an appointment with the architect he'd chosen. Not since the day he realized his trading company was taking off beyond all expectations had he felt this kind of anticipation.

Mitch had grown less enchanted with the idea of seeing a psychiatrist, but David's good mood refused to be dampened—particularly since he was expecting his younger brother to produce results in finding that elusive MG. Sooner or later Mitch would locate the right garage. Maybe it would be today.

An intangible excitement suffused his body at the thought of meeting her again. She might look like Shannon, but in his gut he knew there would be no disappointment this time. Lord. Her smile alone had electrified him.

He met Mitch in the psychiatrist's waiting room, and they were ushered in almost immediately. Introductions followed, and David found himself thinking about Shannon White's double again.

The chemistry had been there for her, too; he was sure of it. He'd heard her breath catch. He was still mesmerized by the charge that lit up her eyes as she gazed at him. She liked what she saw. That kind of attraction couldn't be feigned.

"I'm glad you both came in," Dr. Morton was saying. "David has already given me a little history about your mother over the phone, Mitch."

The mention of his name brought David to the present with a jerk. Dr. Morton had been in conversation with Mitch for several minutes, but David's thoughts had been elsewhere—back at the speedway.

"Before I can help you, I need to know something first. Is racing a hobby for you, or a career?"

David waited to hear his brother's answer to that question. He'd been wondering, too.

"It's my favorite hobby to date."

"What do you do for a living?"

"About twelve years ago, my brother started up a company for day trading on the stock market."

Dr. Morton flashed David a congratulatory smile. "I imagine everyone in the northwest has heard of its success."

David nodded his thanks.

"After college, David hired me to work for him," Mitch informed him.

"Are you doing well?"

"Very."

"So you split your time between your work and your hobby."

"That's about it."

"Tell me some of your future goals."

"I'd like to learn to fly."

"Will that be in addition to racing?"

"No. I've been thinking about finishing out this season, then starting flying lessons next spring."

"What about marriage, children?"

"Well, yeah. Some day."

The doctor eyed David, then Mitch. "Knowing what I do of your mother's history, the loss of your twin brother, I'm afraid I can't be of much help when it's your mother who needs therapy. But the fact that you made an appointment with me shows you're both sensitive to her anxiety.

"There is one thing I can suggest. Call a family council. The three of you need to sit down and talk about the future, like we're doing now. When you let her in on your short- and long-term plans, give her reassurance that you love her and always intend to watch out for her.

"Of course she'll vent. But that's the whole point. She needs to do it out in the open, in front of you *both,* so she can't manipulate one of you behind the other's back. Nothing's going to take away her fear, but doing this could relieve some of the stress that's been building. Try it. Then let's have another session to discuss how it went."

"We'll follow your advice and get back to you, Doctor," David assured him.

"Good. Now, Mitch—if you don't mind waiting outside, I'd like a word with your brother."

He shot David a puzzled glance as he got to his feet. "Sure."

Curious, David asked, "What did you want to talk to me about?"

"I sensed there was something more you needed to discuss."

"What do you mean?"

"You haven't given the bulk of your money and time to create an institute like yours solely to help your mother rid herself of guilt. I'm not doubting your love for her, but there has to be something else. Something that's driving you to make everything right for your family.

"You do the same thing for your brother. He has a lucrative job because of you. You fund his hobbies. No sacrifice is too great. Why is that, David? You're a good-looking, thirty-five-year-old single male. Men ten years younger than you have already married and started families of their own.''

The doctor tapped his fingers on the desk. ''Why not think about what I've said? Maybe by the next time we meet, you'll have sorted some of this through. That's all for now. You can tell Mitch to come in. I'd like to chat alone with him for a few minutes.''

David made no move to get up. ''I'm not gay, in case you thought I might be feeling guilt on that score.''

''Guilt, warranted or not, can come from most any source.''

''You think I'm feeling guilty?''

''I don't know.'' Dr. Morton cocked his head. ''How old were you when your brother died?''

''Nine.''

''And Mitch was two months, you said?''

''Yes.''

''Do you remember anything about it?''

''Yes. In the middle of the night I heard one of the twins crying. The nursery was next to my bedroom. I loved to play with them, so I got up. I thought maybe one of them had lost his bottle. Michael was making the fuss, but he'd finished his.

''I remember taking hold of his fingers, and he stopped crying. There was a little stuffed cow Mother kept on the dresser. I got it down and put it by his hands. Then I went back to bed.

''Early in the morning I heard her cry out for my father. She kept screaming that Michael wasn't breathing. The—'' He had to clear his throat. ''The agony in her voice was the most awful sound I've ever heard.''

Tears sprang to his eyes as remembered pain came flooding back. ''I heard Mitch start to cry, so I got out of bed and ran to the nursery to find out what was going on.

''She was holding Michael's limp body in her arms. She said, 'He's dead! My baby's dead!' My father was frantic. He took the baby and gave it CPR, but Michael didn't revive.

''The emergency medical technicians came. They couldn't find anything wrong with the baby. There…there was an autopsy. The pathologist said Michael had just stopped breathing and died. He said those things happened sometimes. Only God knew why.''

David couldn't talk anymore. Great heaving sobs came out of him. He buried his face in his hands.

''But you thought you knew why, didn't you, David?''

David's palms had gone clammy. ''Yes,'' he whispered. ''If I hadn't given Michael the cow…''

''Twenty-six years is a long time to carry around a guilty secret. Too long for an innocent nine-year-old whose loving actions had nothing to do with his brother's death.

''Like a physician, you've been trying to make everyone better, to fix things. Because you believe you are responsible for depriving the family of its son and brother. It's not a rational belief but it's stayed with you all these years.''

Dr. Morton continued to speak calmly and quietly. ''Unfortunately it's a fact that a SIDS death always leaves behind unanswered questions and fears. There's a big one in your mind. You're unconsciously afraid that if you ever tried to come to someone's rescue again, you might do it wrong and make another unforgivable mistake.

''Marriage has represented too great a risk for you. Yet the irony is that you're the owner of a multimillion-dollar company that does day trading in the stock market, one of the riskiest businesses there is.

''As I said, you've been trying to heal your family—like a physician. But in your case, David, the old admonition, physician, heal thyself, wouldn't be such a bad idea, would it?''

Unable to sit still, David shot to his feet. These were probably the most illuminating fifteen minutes he'd lived through since Michael's death. He took a shuddering breath, then eyed the doctor soberly. ''Thank you.'' He grinned weakly. ''To think I made this appointment to help Mitch and my mother.''

The other man smiled. ''Let's talk about your mother for a minute. Obviously her burden's been heavy. She carried the babies nine months. She was supposed to be the wonderful mother who would do anything to keep her child safe. But Michael wasn't safe—he died. Her role in the marriage was to be a good wife and mother. But in her eyes she failed at both.

"Likewise, your father felt helpless. He was the family's protector. Yet he couldn't bring Michael back to life. Who knows if some lingering sense of guilt was partly to blame for his heart attack?"

David's amazement at the doctor's insight left him speechless.

"When the three of you have that family council, you might talk over these things with your mother if you feel comfortable enough. It'll surprise her to learn she's not the only one who's suffered all these years because of Michael's death.

"Talking together honestly could bring about a new understanding and closeness. Depending on her reaction, you could suggest she get professional help."

David's mind reeled from the information he was only beginning to process. "I can't tell you what this appointment has meant to me." He shook the doctor's hand.

Dr. Morton smiled warmly. "I'm glad you feel that way. Go ahead and send in your brother. Is it all right if I share what we've talked about with him? It might help him."

"Of course," David murmured before leaving the office.

"How come he wants to see me?" Mitch asked defensively when David told him the doctor was waiting.

"Why don't you go in and find out? I'll be waiting for you in the car."

A half hour later, David watched his brother leave the doctor's office. He walked toward the car as if he were in a trance. When he got in and they drove off, there was total silence coming from Mitch's side.

David could relate. He'd had some time alone to think about what had been discussed.

"Mom needs a lot of help!" Mitch blurted at last.

"We all do, Mitch."

His brother's head was lowered. He kept nodding. David suspected he'd been crying.

"Are you all right?"

"Hell, no! Apparently I've been feeling guilty because I survived and Michael didn't. So I've spent my life wondering how afraid I am of death. He says that every time I get into a race car or an airplane, it's a counterphobic reaction—that's what he called it. An attempt to place myself in a death-defying position."

"Why?"

"To prove I'm not afraid."

David shook his head. "I had no idea. I thought it was because you'd been deprived of your twin, and no other relationship had satisfied you. I believed that in your restless search, you turned to one hobby after another."

"Yeah. He brought that up, too." After a slight hesitation, he murmured, "I didn't know about the cow."

"I didn't know you felt guilty about surviving."

"We're both a mess, aren't we?" He laughed through his tears before raising his head.

"You can say that again. Thank God we've got each other!"

"Amen," Mitch muttered. "But can you picture Mother lasting five minutes when she hears what we've got to say? You know she'll fly out of the room and go to bed with a migraine."

"Then we'll lock the doors and have her medicine on hand."

His brother let out a frustrated sound. "You're serious!"

"I didn't pay the doctor two hundred dollars to ignore his advice."

"I'll write you a check for my half."

"Good. How's Sunday afternoon for our talk with her?"

"Make that a week from Sunday. I have to be in Eugene next weekend for a race."

"I'll get away to watch you." He was hoping the woman he'd been looking for would be in the stands. "In the meantime, do you want me to drop you somewhere, or shall I take you back to work?"

"Why don't we make the rounds of a few more garages working on older-model MGs? Who knows? Today we might learn the name of your mystery woman."

"There's nothing I'd like more, but I'm afraid I have an important appointment. Want to come with me?"

"Depends."

"Remember the old Crompton warehouse that was renovated last year?"

"You mean the eyesore some architect turned into that trendy new complex? Yeah. I had a drink with the pit crew in the basement a couple of days ago. A bar called the Pub. The whole place is incredible."

"I couldn't agree more. I had dinner there recently, and I liked what I saw so much, I found out the name of the firm that worked on it. I want Casey & Associates to design a new complex to house the institute."

"Casey? I wonder if that's any relation to Jack Casey."

"I don't know, but I'll find out. I have my first meeting with the architect in twenty minutes."

Mitch whistled. "That could be a marathon event. You'd better take me back home. I'll get my car and try to track down the MG on my lunch hour."

"I'm counting on you, Mitch."

"Yeah, well, I owe you."

David smiled at him. "I like the sound of that."

"I thought you would."

After letting Mitch out in front of his apartment building, David headed for the freeway. As he drove, David's secretary called on his car phone to inform him that the architect he was supposed to meet had gotten tied up with a problem at a new building. Could David join him at the site?

That was fine with him. When he asked if there were any other messages, she gave him a list that included Shannon White's name. The more it kept cropping up, the more he shoved it to the back of his mind.

Right now, it was her sister—her unknown sister—who dominated his world. He wouldn't rest until he'd found her.

It didn't take him long to locate the partially erected six-floor office building in a fashionable suburb of Portland. David was pleased to discover that it displayed the extensive use of wood, joists and exposed joinery, as well as the wide floor-to-ceiling windows he'd come to think of as unique to the firm of Casey & Associates. He pulled his Mercedes to the work fence, grabbed his briefcase and headed for the trailer.

A workman in the distance noticed David and called to him. "Looking for somebody?"

"The architect. I have an appointment."

"Up there." The guy pointed to a figure in a hard hat walking around on one of the steel girders. "You can wait in the trailer or grab a hard hat and ride in the cage."

"Thanks."

"You bet!"

Curious to see a building at this stage of development, David donned a hat and hurried toward the makeshift elevator.

He leased his current office space, so he was excited about building a permanent facility on twenty acres of wooded property he'd purchased six months ago. The land was situated a couple of miles outside

Portland, close enough to the city for convenience, far enough to provide a measure of silence and serenity.

He had a few basic ideas for the kind of design he wanted. But when he'd seen the Crompton warehouse makeover, he'd recognized real genius and found himself looking forward to meeting its creator.

A couple of workmen went up in the cage with him. The sun had come to Portland, at last, and the afternoon heat felt good on David's face. He removed his suit jacket, tossing it over his shoulder.

A fear of heights had never been one of his problems, yet he couldn't help admiring the men who worked on much taller buildings. This might not be a skyscraper or anything close to it, but six floors up was still six floors up.

"Hey, CC?" one of the men shouted. "You've got company!"

"Be right there!"

The person in the hard hat making his way off the girder didn't look anything like the architect David had imagined. For one thing, he didn't walk like a man.

The woman—unmistakably a woman, wearing a white T-shirt and slim blue jeans—moved toward him at a fast pace.

"Hello! I'm Catherine Casey," she called to him, from a distance. "Thanks for meeting me here, but you didn't have to come all the way up. When I saw you get out of your car, I realized you must be my client and I was about to go down to the trailer.''

Only a few feet from him, she extended her hand. ''My secretary must have told me your name, but I confess I don't remember it.'' She lifted her head to smile at him, exactly as she'd done at the speedway.

His heart knocked violently against his chest.

THE STRANGER from the track! Her breath caught in her throat. She felt his fingers tighten around hers, almost as if he couldn't believe the coincidence, either.

''I'm David Britton.''

Britton? She gasped. ''Then it was—''

''Mitch,'' he interrupted her. ''My younger brother.'' She felt his tension when he asked, ''Is Jack Casey your husband?''

''No!'' she cried, then blushed because she knew she'd sounded too eager to clarify the point. ''He's *my* younger brother.''

The coincidences were mounting.

They seemed to comprehend each other's worlds without having to speak another word. She'd never communicated on this level with anyone else.

A smile broke the corners of his mouth. His dark-fringed eyes lit up. They weren't midnight blue, as she'd originally thought. If anything, their color rivaled the waters of Capri's Blue Grotto. She saw no displeasure in them.

''Do I still remind you of the person named Shannon?'' It was vital she get an honest answer to that question right away.

''Only superficially.'' His hand squeezed hers before letting go.

''Would you rather talk in the trailer?''

''No.'' The answer came swiftly. ''The view is fine up here.''

She tried to breathe normally. ''My secretary said you're thinking of building a new office complex.''

''I got past the thinking stage when I saw what you did with the Crompton warehouse.''

Warmth crept through her body. ''That was a fun project.''

''Fun.'' His lips twitched. ''Which do you prefer? A virgin piece of ground or a condemned wreck?''

''Both of the above.''

''Ask a foolish question,'' he muttered before smiling again. ''Are you through here for today?''

That depended on who wanted to know, and for what reason. If she was wrong about *his*...

Her heart pounded in her ears. ''I am.''

''Good. I'd like you to see the property. It's about a twenty-minute drive from here.''

''In which direction?''

''West. Near Cedar Hills.''

The other side of town. ''I'll follow you in my truck.''

He seemed about to say something, then apparently thought the better of it. In a few strides he reached the cage and opened the door. He gave her a long, assessing glance as she stepped past him. They started their descent.

"I heard about the accident at the speedway. How bad were your brother's injuries?"

"He escaped with bruised ribs. By now, I'd say Mitch has used up seven of his nine lives."

"Jack has already started on a new cat!"

He started to laugh, and she joined him. "We drove to the hospital that evening to see if the drivers involved were going to be all right. To our relief, the ER nurse told us everyone had been released."

Something flickered in his eyes. "What time did you get there?"

"Around quarter to eight."

"Mitch and I must have just missed you."

Catherine averted her gaze. *Slow down. Calm down.* "I watched your brother at the race. His red car flew around that track driving everyone else crazy, especially my brother. Jack said Mitch would have won the race if the other car hadn't caught fire and created an accident."

"I guess we'll never know for sure, but there's another race in Eugene this coming weekend."

She could hardly breathe. "I know. Will your brother be able to drive this soon after being injured?"

"Does night follow day?" They arrived at the ground floor with a bounce. He opened the door. She was still smiling when he said, "Come to the race with me."

The thing she'd wanted to happen was happening.

"Do you think our brothers will mind us consorting with the enemy, so to speak?"

He grinned. "If they don't approve of our consorting, I can think of any number of other things we could do. Even discuss business."

"That might work."

"It might interest you to know that Mitch is being paid handsomely to find a certain blonde who ran away from me at the speedway before I could learn her name."

His admission thrilled Catherine. It meant she wasn't the only one affected by their chance meeting.

"That wasn't very nice of her." His voice was level, without inflection. "She didn't even leave a glass slipper. I've told my brother to check with every mechanic in Portland who's ever worked on a vintage-model green MG." All mirth had disappeared.

Catherine trembled because she sensed he wasn't joking. In a quiet voice she said, "My brother's pit crew takes care of my car."

"I figured that out ten minutes ago."

Something was going on here. Something beyond her control. It reminded her of the way she felt when a design took on a life of its own. Yet this was different. This was more.

Everything was going too fast, propelling her toward a level of awareness she couldn't explain. It frightened her. And it excited her.

As she headed for the trailer, he adjusted his long

strides to stay abreast of her. "If you'll give me your hat, I'll put it away," she told him.

When he pulled it off, she tried not to stare at the varying shades of wavy brown illuminated by the sun. He had healthy hair defined by a slight widow's peak. The arrangement of strong masculine features, the lines of experience around his nose and mouth, made him an exceptionally attractive man.

Careful to keep her eyes down, she removed her hard hat and tossed both hats in the bin beside the door. The foreman on the project looked up from his desk.

"You're leaving?"

"That's right. I'll come around again on Monday, Sol. If anybody needs to get hold of me, I can be reached on the cell phone. I'm driving out to look at a new building site and should be home in a couple of hours."

How many times in her career had she said those exact words to a foreman or workman? Yet this afternoon they meant something entirely different.

This day wasn't like any other.

This client wasn't like any other.

"Shall we go in one car?" David enquired.

"It might be better if I followed you. I have an appointment downtown after our meeting. But thank you for offering."

He nodded, then walked her to her truck. He opened the door and helped her inside.

What was perhaps most surprising was the fact that she let him. It had been years since she'd lowered her guard to this degree, years since she'd allowed anyone to treat her as anything other than a boss or one of the guys. Was it because he'd taken up residence in her mind? She'd been dreaming about him, and she remembered her dream images clearly—although that had hardly ever happened in the past.

As she sat behind the wheel of the truck, her eyes were almost even with his.

His expression sobered. "Drive carefully."

Coming from anyone else, the warning might not have carried the same weight. But Catherine understood. Those were the same words the family told Jack before he left for a race.

Life was always precious, but never more so than now.

"You, too," she whispered.

CHAPTER THREE

RELIEVED TO DISCOVER that she didn't drive with her brother's unconscious death wish, David reached for his cell phone and punched in his brother's number.

"Hello?"

"Mitch?"

"Hey—give a guy a break! I haven't had time to visit more than two garages since you dropped me off!"

"That's why I'm calling. The woman in question has been found. Since I haven't paid you for the hours you've put in, and you'll never pay me for the psychiatric visit, why don't we call it even?"

"It's a deal. Hey…you sound happy!"

"That's the understatement of a lifetime."

"A lifetime? Those are strong words. What did you do, crash into her or something?" He laughed.

"Remember Crompton's warehouse?"

"Not that again…"

"She designed its makeover. I'll get back to you later."

"Wait—"

David shut off the phone. He wasn't ready to talk to anyone about this yet, not even Mitch.

It might be rude to stare at her through the rear-view mirror, but he didn't care. After finding her, he wasn't about to let her out of his sight.

The daughter, not the father, had turned out to be CC Casey, architect extraordinaire.

And the other daughter? The unknown sister?

No matter how much David didn't want to think about Shannon, she insisted upon intruding on his consciousness.

Would she have become an architect instead of a nurse if she'd been reared by Catherine's architect father, too?

How much of a role did environment play in their behavior?

Or did the fact that Shannon was a nurse prove what the gene studies at his lab were suggesting—that identical twins were rarely truly identical?

David knew he was oversimplifying things. But he couldn't help wondering about the disparate traits, the convergence of various individual attitudes, in each of the women. It was hard to define exactly what they were, these qualities, but they'd killed his initial interest in Shannon, yet made Catherine more desirable to him than any woman he'd ever met.

While he pondered those intangible differences, he found himself wondering why the Caseys had given up one of their twins for adoption in the first place. How did they decide which daughter to keep?

Had they kept it a secret from Catherine?

If she didn't know she had a twin, then David had

no legal or moral right to divulge that information, even if Shannon was searching for her.

Since unburdening himself to the doctor, David had been feeling immeasurably better about the past. Now it seemed he was caught in a new moral dilemma. The happiness and welfare of numerous lives were at stake here, including his own.

He certainly hadn't meant to hurt Shannon by starting and then immediately ending something that wasn't meant to be. However, he'd hoped that if she did have a twin, she'd be successful in finding him or her.

It had been her dream that her unknown sister or brother would answer the institute's ad, providing a means by which they'd be united. But if Catherine had been kept in the dark all these years, then there was no way the twin studies project could be the catalyst to bring about a meeting of the two sisters. That wasn't the institute's function.

His responsibility to Shannon began and ended with information obtained through their database. Without any involvement on Catherine's part, there would be no information. In that case, he'd be forced by the precariousness of the situation to close the book on Shannon.

So far, she'd shown no sign of giving up on a romantic relationship with him. If anything, her determination to be with him seemed more intense than ever, evidenced by the message she'd left with his secretary earlier today.

David had never known a woman who wouldn't

take no for an answer. Sometimes he felt Shannon's behavior bordered on the abnormal, but maybe that was putting it too strongly. She was compulsive, anyway, and oddly insensitive to the desires of other people.

It was inconceivable to him that he could have such diametrically opposing thoughts and feelings about sisters who'd come from the same fertilized egg and been born exact copies of each other.

Yet it was a fact.

Unless, or until, Catherine revealed that she believed or knew she had an identical twin and wanted to find her sibling, David had no choice but to keep any knowledge of Shannon's relationship to her a secret.

Earlier, when Catherine had asked him about the person named Shannon, he hadn't sensed anything in her question beyond natural curiosity. Furthermore, she'd seemed happy with his answer. Therefore he was letting the matter go. In his heart he rejoiced that he could.

Since the day she'd bumped into him at the speedway, he'd wrestled with his conscience. But no longer. That was all in the past—unless Catherine indicated some awareness of a twin. He sensed, somehow, that she wouldn't.... He doubted she had any idea.

Starting now, he was free to discover what there could be between him and the exciting woman driving right behind him. As they took the Skybridge route through Cedar Hills, he vowed that he wouldn't let anything or anyone get in his way.

CATHERINE WATCHED David approach the truck. She had dreamed about this man, and he seemed uncannily familiar to her, yet the reality of being in his physical presence made it almost impossible to concentrate. She knew she had a job to do, but her legs felt as insubstantial as jelly, and her heart fluttered all over the place.

Designing a new building in the middle of a busy metropolis presented many challenges. But here, nature had already supplied the aesthetic framework, and pictures of the finished product flooded Catherine's mind. The abundance of evergreens covering David Britton's twenty acres of land sent out images like a beacon transmitting signals.

He'd helped her from the cab, and they took a leisurely walk. David related nothing more than the dimensions of the twenty-acre lot. Once again, their minds seemed to communicate what was important.

Finally, Catherine said, "This is a choice piece of property. Tell me what's going to go on inside the building you envision here."

She listened attentively as he explained, taking deliberate pains not to look at him. It was distracting enough to be standing within touching distance.

When he'd finished talking about a subject that appeared to consume him, she said, "You mentioned earlier that you were impressed with the Crompton warehouse renovation. Does this mean you pictured your institute offices, clinic and lab under one roof?''

''I hadn't thought that far. The only thing I can tell you is that you achieved something superb with that warehouse.''

The sincerity of his tone thrilled her. ''Thank you. Perhaps one of the reasons you liked it so much was because it was *meant* to invite. I had certain walls removed and replaced by curving glass to make the lines of the building flow, to draw the viewer in. As well, every shop and restaurant inside the edifice provides a particular service to the public. Therefore it required an all-of-a-piece look to say that no one part was more important than the other. To do a good job, the design should enhance the function.

''In the case of your institute, you have several functions going on, most of which are not shared with the general public. For example, the lab houses scientific experimentation, which is off-limits to anyone except authorized personnel and the subjects being tested.

''There's the main business section, where the staff handles phone, computer and Internet correspondence. That, too, is off-limits. You have meeting and consultation rooms, and a library. Then there's your own private suite of offices, which ought to be separately maintained.

''From what I've gathered, the only time you deal with the public is when people drop in to be interviewed or arrive for their consultations and tests.

''To this point, everything's been housed under

one roof, making it impossible to delineate all the different functions, either physically or psychologically. Not only that, when you first took out your lease, you hadn't grown to the proportions you've reached today, and now you're working on top of each other, so to speak. Have I missed anything?''

''No.'' He shook his head slowly. ''In fact you've just solved the mystery of why my frustration level has been at an all-time high.''

She chuckled. ''If you'd ever seen drawings of the city of London in the making, you'd notice there was little rhyme or reason to the way it was designed. In fact, you couldn't really say it *was* designed. Everything sort of came together in a hodgepodge. I'm afraid our working worlds aren't much different.

''But once in a while there's a person like you who has the vision and luxury of building something from scratch. A creation that will make perfect sense and appeal to the eye, as well.''

He nodded slowly.

''Tell me, David, have you ever visited a Zulu village?''

She heard the slight hesitation before he said, ''I'm sorry to say I haven't.''

Catherine darted him an amused glance. ''I visited once, but don't worry. I'm just thinking about the layout, although authentic zebra skins and spears do add the right touch in their proper ambience.''

He laughed, then gestured for her to continue.

''The huts of the particular village I visited

formed a circle, with the chief's hut in the center. The villagers had their work and relationships figured out and created something beautifully simple, yet completely functional.

"That's what I see here. A roughly circular series of buildings, all suited to their own special jobs, connected by paths where more trees and flowering shrubs will be planted to provide natural cover from the elements. There's plenty of room for hidden parking areas, which can be placed for staff convenience.

"We'll fit the buildings into the landscape as if they'd sprung up naturally, and incorporate cedar siding by using it on the exteriors. I'd like to experiment with various wood inlays to provide shades of richness and texture.

"Of course, this is just an idea. I'll make several renderings for you, including a conventional building. Keep in mind that containing everything under one roof will make your complex obsolete within a year or two, because various aspects of your business will continue to grow.

"The beauty of the village concept is adaptation. In this Garden of Eden setting you'll have the room to expand, and the effect will remain appropriate and attractive.

"You'll also make a statement that says you have an affinity with the environment. You'll have created a timeless sylvan elegance at peace with nature from the chaos of a tumultuous twenty-first century."

Sometimes after a stirring operatic or symphonic performance, there was a hush in the audience before it burst into applause. Was that what David's silence meant? Was it arrogant to hope so? At the very least, she hoped he'd grasped the essence of what she'd tried to convey and felt excited about it.

"How do you do it?" His voice was hushed.

"Do what?"

"It has to be a gift."

Her face felt warm. "I went to school."

"You were born a genius. But that's not what I'm talking about." He moved closer. "In a matter of seconds you've summed up thoughts and feelings inside me that *I've* never even articulated before."

Now that she knew she was on the right track, she could release the breath she'd been holding. "When I can get someone to talk about the thing he's passionate about, then it's easy to see into his soul. A good architect wants the end product to reflect his client's psyche.

"In your case, the new institute will stand as a personal monument to hard work, sacrifice and the greater good of the community. I'm very impressed."

She noticed the sudden heaving of his chest. "Have dinner with me tonight," he said quietly.

"I'd like that." She struggled to keep her voice steady. "But it's my mom's birthday. Dad's taking the family to her favorite seafood restaurant, and I still haven't picked up her present yet."

His eyes narrowed. "Then we won't be able to see each other until Saturday."

She turned her face away, afraid her expression would reveal how endless five more days sounded.

"What's the best way to reach you that guarantees I can speak to you personally?"

"My cell phone."

He pulled out a notebook and jotted down her number, then escorted her to the truck. "We'll have to get an early start to beat the traffic to Eugene on Saturday morning." Once she was inside the cab, he shut the door. "I'll call you Friday to make final arrangements."

Don't act too excited, Catherine. "By then I ought to have a few preliminary sketches for you to look over."

"I'm not going anywhere, so there's no rush. Now I understand why you're in such high demand. I feel privileged to have been taken on as a client."

She shook her head. "I'm the one who's privileged. To be asked to create something that will live up to a client's expectations is an awesome responsibility."

"You've already surpassed mine, and there's nothing down on paper yet. Good night, Catherine Casey. Enjoy your party."

This time he followed her until they reached downtown Portland, where he disappeared. It was a good thing an important family celebration had prevented her from accepting his dinner invitation. She needed a few days and some distance to understand why she was running toward him instead of retreating the way she usually did.

While she was in the Brushworks Gallery to collect the Van Gogh print she'd had framed for her mother, her thoughts leaped ahead to the weekend. She'd be spending all of Saturday with David. Until then, she'd try not to think about him. But, of course, that was ridiculous, since just moments ago she'd promised to present him with drawings the next time they met.

SHANNON HAD DRIVEN down from Tacoma early, hoping to catch sight of David, but so far no luck. She'd been waiting over an hour. The woman at the front desk probably wondered what was going on.

Maybe something had held him up, or else he wasn't coming in at all. Full of disappointment, she approached the receptionist, whose nameplate indicated that her name was Barbara Ross.

"Could I speak to someone in personnel?"

"May I ask why? Perhaps I can help you."

"I'd like to apply for a job here."

"At present we're not looking for anyone to hire."

"Could I at least have an application in case there's an opening?"

"Of course. Just a minute, please." The receptionist walked over to a file cabinet along the wall and pulled a packet from the drawer. "Here you are. When you've filled it in, mail it to the address at the top."

"If you don't mind, Barbara, I'd like to complete it while I'm here."

"That's fine. You can use this clipboard and sit down over there."

"Thank you." Shannon studied the forms.

The Britton Institute of Genetic Research on Twins
65 Columbia Drive, Portland, Oregon
Application Form

Name: Shannon White

Age: 28
(optional)

Marital Status: Single
(optional)

Address: 4973 Southeast 116th
Place, Tacoma,
Washington

Telephone: Home phone
253–555–2109
Work phone
253–555–5320

Qualifications: I have a Masters Degree in Nursing from the University of Washington, and am currently Administrator of Nursing at Glen Cove Nursing Home, a one-hundred-bed facility in Tacoma, Washington. I have worked for three years. For personal reasons, I am planning to move to Portland whenever the right job becomes available.

Before I joined the staff at Glen Cove, I was the administrator of a health care facility for Haida Indians on Prince of Wales Island in Alaska for a year. I've written several papers, which have been published in the *American Journal of Nursing*.

Position applied for: I am applying for work at your institute as an administrator to help coordinate the data you're accumulating on identical twins.

Why do you want to work here? About a month ago, I saw the institute's ad in the paper, and drove down from Tacoma to participate in your twin studies project. I came because shortly before her death, my adoptive mother said something about my being a twin.

I didn't know if her pain medication had caused her to hallucinate or if she decided she didn't want to go to her grave with a secret that important. Since I am my deceased parents' only child, and have no living relatives, it's possible she wanted me to search out my twin so I wouldn't be left alone.

If he or she exists, perhaps the institute will be the means of bringing us together. I've explained this to let you know of my interest and desire to work for such a worthy cause.

References: With this application I include my transcripts of credits for both undergraduate and graduate school, five letters of recommendation, copies of my published articles and a recent photograph.

"Excuse me, Barbara. I've finished filling out the application. Will you please file this envelope of documents with it?"

"Certainly."

"Tell me something."

"Yes?"

"A month ago Mr. Britton interviewed me when I answered the ad to be a participant in the study. Does he also do the hiring of personnel?"

"He has the ultimate say."

"Will you make sure he sees this?"

"Of course."

"Thank you very much."

She waited another half hour, then gave up and decided to do more job-hunting. As long as she was in Portland, it would be foolish to waste any more time hoping he might come back to his office.

FRIDAY AFTERNOON had arrived at last!

David finished putting his signature to the last of a stack of letters. He couldn't get out of his office fast enough. The long wait was almost over.

Anyone might have thought he was a besotted younger man unable to focus on anything but the beautiful woman in his life. As soon as he got home, he'd phone Catherine. Since the day they'd been to look at his property, he'd been living to hear her voice again.

He buzzed his secretary. "Louise? The correspondence is ready to be mailed. I'm leaving now. I'll be out of town all day tomorrow. If an emergency arises over the weekend, I can be reached on my cell phone. Otherwise I'll see you Monday."

"Yes, sir. But before you go, there's something I think you should see. I'll be right in."

She met him at the door to his office. "I realize you're in a hurry to get away, but you did tell me to let you know if Shannon White ever came to the institute again."

At the mention of her name, David's anger flared. He took a steadying breath. "Is she out in reception?"

"No, but apparently she was in earlier this week. Barbara received an employment application from her. She put it in my basket, and I just got to it. Barbara left a note with it.

"It seems Ms. White told her that you'd interviewed her when she answered the ad to become a participant. Barbara thought perhaps you'd suggested there might be an opening at the institute, particularly since Ms. White has such excellent skills and qualifications. She brought transcripts and letters of recommendation with her."

David already knew Shannon's qualifications. But he was only beginning to comprehend her skill at manipulation. Not for the first time did he regret taking her out to dinner. That one kiss had turned out to be the biggest mistake he'd ever made where a woman was concerned.

His lapse in judgment had given Shannon an edge. Unfortunately she was continuing to use it to full advantage. She knew that mentioning David's name would compel Barbara to pass her application directly to him. His growing lack of interest in Catherine's twin had just taken a leap toward true aversion.

"Thanks for bringing it to my attention, but you can discard it. We're not hiring anyone right now. Even if a position were to open up in the future, you might remind Barbara—and the staff in personnel—that it's against company policy to engage the services of anyone who's a participant in the project."

"Yes, sir."

"Tell Barbara something else. If Ms. White should show her face again, and she probably will when she doesn't hear back from us, Barbara should call me. I'll walk over and deal with the woman myself."

"I'll speak to her before I leave tonight."

"Thanks, Louise. Have a nice weekend."

"You, too, Mr. Britton."

I intend to.

As he made his way to the underground car park, he refused to let Shannon's manipulations infringe on his life or his pleasure with Catherine.

He'd backed his car halfway out of his slot when the cell phone rang. There was no need to look at the caller ID. The day before one of Mitch's races guaranteed their mother would end up in bed with a migraine. Today was no different. He'd swing by to see her on his way home.

AFTER EVERYONE ELSE in the office had gone for the weekend, Catherine was still at her drafting table. Normally the quiet hours of late afternoon proved to be her most productive. But she'd been waiting for one particular call all day and hadn't been able to settle down to business with her usual amount of concentration.

Maybe some emergency had arisen, preventing David from phoning. Any minute she expected him to call and cancel their plans for tomorrow. She kept telling herself it wouldn't be the end of the world. But the searing disappointment she experienced every time she contemplated the possibility let her know otherwise.

When her cell phone finally rang, she forced herself to remain calm, letting it ring three times before answering. Then she looked at her caller ID and saw Jack's cell phone number. Much as she loved her brother, Catherine's spirits plummeted.

"Hello, Jack."

"It's Melanie!" A bright voice spoke the words. "We're in Eugene. Jack's talking to the crew right now, so I thought I'd phone to see if you're going to make it tomorrow."

Catherine hadn't told them about her date with David, or even that she'd actually met him. For that matter, she didn't know if David had chosen to tell Mitch, either.

In case their plan fell through, it might be better not to say anything. David hadn't phoned yet. If her fears were borne out, she'd have to drive to Eugene by herself.

"I'm working late so I can be free tomorrow to watch the whole thing."

"That's great. Jack says no one else in your family will be able to make it. Brody's in-laws came to town unexpectedly."

"What about Mark?"

"According to Jack, he's in Astoria getting some depositions on a law case."

"Melanie, as long as Jack's got you, he's happy. I'm sorry to say Mom's big fund-raiser for the Women in Distress shelter has its opener tomorrow. Dad promised to help her. But I'll be there. I'm bringing the camcorder to get his victory on tape."

"I brought my camcorder, too. Plan to sit with me. I'll save you a place."

"I'll find you. Tell Jack God bless."

"Don't worry." Melanie's voice held a distinct tremor.

Catherine admired Melanie as much as she liked her. It would be hard to be in love with a race car driver, hard to act happy and confident when you feared for his life every time he got behind the wheel.

As she ended the conversation, Catherine's gaze fell on the drawings she'd made for David. A few more details and they'd be finished. She searched for a portfolio and packed them away. She'd take them home to finish; that way, they'd be ready if she did see him tomorrow.

No sooner had she started for the door than her cell phone rang again. This time she didn't stop to compose herself, let alone see who was calling. As a result, she sounded breathless when she said hello.

"Catherine?"

At the sound of his deep voice she felt suddenly weak and leaned against the doorjamb for support. "Hello, David."

"Sorry I haven't called before now. After working all hours to clear my desk today, I found out my mother needed to see me, but I'll explain about that in the morning. Can you be ready at seven? I'd like to take you to breakfast on our way out of town."

"Seven sounds fine."

"Mitch guessed I'm bringing you with me. He can hardly wait to be introduced."

She smiled. "I'm looking forward to meeting the only guy who can beat Jack."

"Maybe. But racing isn't Mitch's consuming passion, like it's Jack's. With every hobby, he eventually burns out. Then it's on to a new one. That, by the way, is a secret between you and me."

"Of course." Jack would be overjoyed if he heard such news. "You've relieved me of a big worry, but rest assured, I'll never tell. If Jack knew the truth, it would make him overconfident. Then he'd lose his edge."

"Mitch has connections with a lot of people in

the racing business. From what he tells me, your brother could go right to the top.''

"That's very generous of him. If Jack can amass enough winnings and financial support—and if he continues to hone his skills—maybe one day he'll get there. It's all he's dreamed about since his teens. Our family's a hundred percent behind him.''

"Then he can't lose.''

"I don't know. Jack says Mitch Britton is the guy to beat tomorrow.''

"It's going to be an exciting day all around.''

I know.

"Where are you right now?''

She sucked in her breath. "I'm just leaving my office with your drawings in hand.''

"After we get back from Eugene, I'd like to sit down and look at them. Now, what's your address?''

She gave him directions to her condo, which was in an older building that had once housed apartments. "Number six. Use the lobby phone and I'll let you in.''

"My condo's three blocks from yours. That's a plus I hadn't counted on. See you in the morning, Catherine.''

Only three?

That meant they must have driven past each other dozens of times on their way to or from someplace else. "I'll be waiting.'' She hurriedly hung up so he couldn't hear her heart hammering out of control.

CHAPTER FOUR

SHANNON LOOKED AROUND the crowded room of the Crompton Steakhouse. She knew it was foolish, but when she hadn't been able to catch David at his work last week, she hoped she might run into him here.

He'd raved about the architecture of the warehouse and had seemed to like this restaurant a lot. Since it was a Friday night, he could be dining here. The institute hadn't phoned or written about either the project or the job application. Maybe talking to him in person would make the difference, at least as far as a job was concerned.

"Good evening. Again!"

She lifted her head. The waiter looked vaguely familiar. "Hello."

"I'm Steve. I waited on you before."

"Oh, yes."

"Shall I bring you what you ordered last time or do you want a menu?"

"You must have a photographic memory if you can remember that far back. Tell me what I had."

"Filet mignon well done, champignons, a baked potato and salad with vinegar and oil dressing."

"That's very impressive, except for two details. I

like my steak medium rare, and you left out the raspberry sorbet. But I forgive you.''

''Wait a minute— Then you're the one who came in the first time!''

''What are you talking about? I've only been here once before.''

''Yes, I know that now. But I got mixed up because your double was in here recently. She ordered the same meal, except she wanted her steak well done.''

Shannon's body stilled. ''What do you mean, my double?''

''That's exactly what she asked me when I mistook her for you!''

''You thought we looked like the same person?''

''You want to know something?'' he said in a confiding tone. ''I was friends with a pair of identical twins all through school. Most of the time, the teachers and students got so mixed up, they called them by the wrong names. I never got them right, either.

''I'm telling you, if that other woman was sitting next to you, I wouldn't be able to guess which one of you wanted the steak well done and which one wanted it rare. Like I told her, you guys are identical. You must be related and don't know it,'' he said excitedly.

''She didn't question you about it when you told her?''

''No.'' He paused. ''I don't think she took my comment literally.''

"That probably means she doesn't know she has a twin who's searching for her. But *I* know."

She sat bolt upright. "Listen, Steve, before my adoptive mother died she said something about my being a twin. But she was so ill, I didn't know whether to believe her or not. Still, I've been looking for a brother or sister ever since.

"What you've just told me means my mother was telling the truth. Please—I need your help. Do you remember her name or the name of the person with her?"

"No."

"Did they pay cash?"

He thought for a minute. "No. A credit card."

"Do you think you could find a copy of it and give me the information so I can look her up?"

He shook his head. "Even if I could find it, it would be illegal."

She bit her lip. "Listen, I'm going to leave you my picture and my business card. It has my home and work numbers on it. If she should come in here again, tell her about me, show her this picture and get a phone number from her. Then call me collect. Will you do it? Please?"

He blinked. "Sure."

"You have no idea what this means to me." She got up from the table.

"Aren't you going to eat?"

"I couldn't. Not now." She pulled some bills from her purse. "Here's twenty for dinner and twenty for your help. I'm counting on you."

He looked surprised. "If I ever see her in here again, believe me, I'll find out everything I can and let you know."

"Thanks, Steve."

His admiring gaze swept over her. "You're welcome. Anytime."

Her feet hardly touched the ground as she left the restaurant. So her twin *did* exist! This was something she needed to share with David. She was overjoyed because it gave her a legitimate reason to see him again.

THE EARLY JULY HEAT brought spectators to the Eugene speedway in droves. David was glad of the crowded bleachers. While Melanie Barlow, Jack's vivacious brunet girlfriend, was in another world as she followed his progress around the track, David had been searching for any excuse to touch Catherine.

In the car they'd been too far apart. But here, with so many people packed together, she'd been forced to sit close to him. He was aware of every breath she took.

Beneath her dusky-blue shirt and black cotton pants, he felt the feminine warmth of her arms, the provocative curve of her hips and shapely legs. Though he'd come to the track to support his brother, David found himself captivated by her *joie de vivre*. Before he'd met her, it was the same quality he'd seen in her architecture.

She seemed to embrace the essence of the day,

the best part. He'd never met a woman more vital and alive. Her excitement about life was reflected in her eyes, her smile, her conversation.

Though she wasn't conscious of it, David could feel her charm distill over him like a fine mist. Already he was dreading the moment when he had to say good night to her.

Throughout the race, she'd been sharing her binoculars with him. But now that it was nearing the last few minutes, he refused them so she could watch her brother's progress to the end.

Over breakfast, David had learned enough to understand the importance of every win for Jack Casey, not only in points but in prize money so he could build his formula one car.

Catherine jumped to her feet, but still held onto David's hand. "It doesn't look like either of our brothers is going to come in first today."

"One of his sponsors asked Jack to try out some new tires for this race," Melanie informed them. "They've given him nothing but trouble. I bet he could kick himself now. Uh-oh. It's over. Number thirty won." She lowered the binoculars. A look of disappointment appeared on her lovely face.

David stood behind Catherine as the checkered flags were waved. "The doctor warned Mitch to rest his bruised ribs," he murmured, his hands on her shoulders. He couldn't stop touching her. "He drove well, but I could tell he's not up to par yet."

Catherine turned to gaze into his eyes. "I don't know about Mitch, but after a loss, my brother goes into a real decline. Thank heaven for Melanie," she whispered.

Her tremulous voice drove him to put a comforting arm around her shoulders. The gesture disturbed the back of her sun-warmed hair, and he could smell the flowery scent of her shampoo. He inhaled deeply.

"Mitch handles defeat reasonably well, but then he doesn't have as much at stake as your brother. Why don't we take them both out to dinner?" At her enthusiastic nod, he said, "Let's go out to the car and drive to the other side of the speedway to find them. Melanie?" he asked the other woman. "Are you ready?"

"Oh, yes."

"Catherine and I were thinking it might be a good idea if we all went out to dinner. It ought to lighten everyone's mood before we head home."

Melanie beamed. "Jack will love that. Since they both lost, they can commiserate. Before long, they'll be consoling each other and planning their strategies for the next race."

As Melanie hurried ahead of them, Catherine flashed him that glorious smile of hers. "Thank you."

"For what?"

She stared at him long and hard. "For making this a wonderful day, for being so thoughtful and generous, for saying the right things at the right time, for being willing to cheer up Melanie. It'll mean a lot to Jack. It means a lot to me."

Her words went soul deep. There were a lot of things he would've liked to say in response, but this wasn't the time or place. "You know something? This wonderful day is far from over. Come on."

He cupped her elbow, and they left the bleachers as fast as the crowds would allow. The feeling of togetherness was so strong, he could barely remember what it was like *not* to feel this way. He'd never experienced such a sense of wholeness. Of completion.

As soon as they reached the car, he helped her and Melanie inside, then they were off. There was always a mad scramble in the parking area after any race. Used to the chaos, David swung wide to avoid potential accidents and circled the speedway.

When he saw members of his brother's crew, he began honking. Mitch had to be in the middle of the swarm. "There he is. The one in the red racing suit with the Citrus Surprise logo. Notice how he's carrying his crash helmet. Obviously his ribs are still too sore for him to tuck it under his arm."

Catherine's gaze fastened on the younger man walking toward them. "Except for being smaller, he looks so much like you, I can't believe it."

"Well, well." A voice filtered in through the open window. "You stayed for the whole nine yards to watch my demise." He leaned down and gave David a punch on the shoulder.

"Catherine, this is my younger brother, Mitch Britton. Mitch, allow me to introduce you to Catherine Casey, Jack Casey's sister."

His brother's face had broken into a grin. David could see the male admiration in his gaze when it fell on Catherine.

"I've been wanting to meet the owner of the sporty little MG I've been looking for all over town."

"Mitch, I'd also like you to meet Melanie Barlow, Jack Casey's girlfriend."

"I've seen you around. Nice to meet you." They shook hands.

"You're a superb driver, Mitch," Catherine offered.

"Coming from Jack Casey's sister, that's a compliment I'm going to have emblazoned on my helmet."

She laughed. "I'm sorry only one person could win out there today."

"Aren't we all." He groaned.

David smiled at his brother. "The three of us are going to take you two losers out to dinner. Why don't you peel off that monkey suit and come with us? We'll bring you back here later to pick up your car."

Mitch eyed Catherine, then David. "Sounds terrific. I'm starving."

"We are, too. Tell you what. We'll come back here in a minute. We have to find Jack."

"He's over there being mobbed. I'll get him!" Melanie cried. "We'll follow you in his Porsche."

A few minutes after she'd vanished into the throng, Mitch climbed in the back seat, minus the suit. "If you don't have a particular place in mind, the Cowboy Grub, about five blocks south of here, serves great ribs. All you can eat."

Catherine turned her head to look at him again. She still couldn't get over it. Despite the difference in their size and age, he bore a remarkable likeness to David. "Jack will enjoy that."

He grinned. "I know."

"Something tells me all you racers ate dinner there last night, and breakfast this morning."

Mitch leaned forward and clasped David on the shoulder. "Hey, she's smart, too."

David didn't say anything, but there was such intimacy in his gaze that she averted her eyes.

"There's no mystery, Mitch," she explained. "It's a well-known fact that race car drivers love good food—and they're remarkably consistent in their habits. When Jack finds something he likes, he doesn't deviate. Growing up, he ate tuna fish sandwiches every day for lunch."

"Yeah? I was a bologna-and-cheese man."

"You still are," David said.

"It'll make my wife's grocery shopping easier."

Catherine saw David's lips quirk. "So, Mitch, have you chosen this particular moment to make an announcement?"

"Nope. I'm waiting for yours first."

David's hand tightened on Catherine's. On cue, a blush washed over her face. Satisfied by that response, he started the car and began driving toward the road leading out of the speedway. In the rearview mirror he could see Jack's Porsche following them.

TOO SOON, Catherine noticed the sign for the Cowboy Grub. David had to let go of her hand to make the turn into the parking lot. All through the day, she'd thrived on the constant contact with him. Crowded into the bleachers as they'd been, she'd had the perfect excuse to lean against his arm.

More often than not, she'd discovered binoculars trained on him. There were too many women at the track eyeing his face and hard-muscled body. A brown Levi's shirt with the sleeves rolled up and well-fitting tan chinos revealed a casual sense of style—and didn't hide his attractions. The other women's brazen attention brought out Catherine's possessive instincts. She didn't like the idea of David attending another race without her.

He escorted her into the packed restaurant. She thought they'd have a long wait, but he took the hostess aside. Before she knew it, they were being shown to a table. Mitch joked about his brother always having that effect on women.

A few moments later, Jack and Melanie joined them.

"Jack," Catherine said. "I'd like you to meet David Britton. He's the man I bumped into at the speedway last week. I'm going to design his office complex. Of course, you've already met his brother, Mitch. David? This is my brother Jack Casey."

As they shook hands, David murmured, "You're

a fine driver, Jack. I expect one day you'll be a household name like Unser or Andretti.''

"Thank you. But after my performance today, maybe I'd better go back to racing my miniature car in the Boy Scouts Pinewood Derby.''

"Jack!'' Melanie burst out laughing.

"You were in Scouts, too?'' Mitch asked.

Jack nodded. "Oh, yeah. I used to load those critters with weights.''

"Mitch did the same thing,'' David told him. "Everyone accused him of cheating.''

"It was the only way to win.''

At Mitch's comment, Jack laughed.

Catherine felt David's hand caress her back. Getting the two brothers together was an even better idea than they'd thought.

She noticed the covert way Jack studied David across the table. In a minute, he sent Catherine a private glance, giving her his nod of brotherly approval.

"You like to fly?'' Mitch asked Jack as soon as the waitress had taken their orders.

"Sometimes I wish my Chevy had wings.''

"I'm talking a Cessna or Piper Cherokee.''

"The smallest plane I've ever been in is a 747. What's it like?''

"A damn sight better than racing.''

"That's hard to believe, isn't it, honey?'' Jack gave Melanie a kiss on the cheek.

The three of them became more engrossed in their private conversation, and David pulled Catherine closer to him. The gesture charged her system with new energy. She didn't have to look at David to know he was pleased by their brothers' friendliness.

Well into the meal, Jack addressed David. "I understand it was the renovation of the Crompton warehouse that first interested you in my sister's work."

"You're right. I figured anyone with that kind of talent could design something unique for me. When I first met her at the site of her latest project in the suburbs, it struck me again that she possesses a rare gift. In fact, the whole Casey family seems to have many talents. When's the next race for you guys?"

"Portland speedway in two weeks."

"Catherine and I were hoping we'd have to drive out of town again."

Melanie hung on to Jack's arm. "There's one in Vancouver next month."

David signaled to the waitress that she should give him the bill. "Then we'll definitely be there."

Before long, the five of them left the restaurant. After thanking David profusely, Jack and Melanie left the parking lot in his Porsche. It didn't take any time at all for David to reach the speedway again.

Once Mitch had picked up his car, David headed for the freeway leading north. Then he turned his head to glance at Catherine. "Alone at last. Come here."

Catherine sat as close to him as the seat belts and gearshift allowed. Her hand seemed to have become a permanent part of his.

"I haven't had such a good time in years."

"Neither have I," she confessed "Mitch is so cute."

David chuckled. "He hates that word."

"So does Jack. But it's an apt description that fits both of them."

"You're right. I like your brother, too. Melanie seems to be mellow enough to handle his intensity."

"She's terrific with him. I'm hoping they'll get married."

"Tell me about your other brothers."

"Well, neither of them is as complex as Jack. They both married in their early twenties, have solid careers and go home to their wives and children at five o'clock every night."

"How much older are they than you?"

"Mark's thirty-three, five years my senior. Brody's the oldest. He's thirty-five."

"And then there's Jack."

"Yes. Until Melanie, he never showed the slightest interest in getting married. He loves to tinker with cars and he keeps horrendous hours. Jack's the kind of person who pushes himself to the edge, no matter what he's doing."

"You love him."

"I do. We're only two years apart. Mom and Dad couldn't have children of their own so they adopted Mark and Brody. Later on, they wanted a bigger family and adopted me.

"Mom says that when they realized I didn't have a playmate, they decided they'd better adopt another little girl. Since none were available, they had to wait. Then Jack came along. We were raised like twins. I've always felt we had a special bond.''

"After what you've told me about being adopted, I find I have to revise my thinking.''

"In what way?''

"I thought you'd come by your architectural talent through your father. Now that I know differently, it makes me wonder whether you inherited that particular gift from one of your birth parents.''

"You sound like my brother, but it doesn't surprise me, not when genetic research is what your institute does." She shook her head. "Of the four of us, Jack's the only one who's ever wanted to find his birth parents. It annoys him that I have no interest in mine.''

"Has he looked for them?''

"Yes. But so far he's been unsuccessful. Personally, I think it's better not to know. Mom and Dad are so loving and wonderful, I can't imagine anyone else being my parents. We've had the best life any children could have been given.

"To be honest, I don't *want* to know anything else. Something tells me that whatever I found out would be unpleasant, maybe even shocking. I have no desire to invite pain when my life is perfect the way it is.

"Jack, of course, has a completely different take on it. He wants to know who his ancestors were, and he talks a lot about the other biological brothers or sisters he might have.

"I've got all the family I want. But that's my brother for you. As long as I've known him, he's been the one to push the limits, so I guess I shouldn't be surprised that he has questions about his origins."

"Are your parents aware he's searching?"

"Yes. They've tried to help him."

"They sound like terrific people."

"They are." She stifled a yawn. "I can't wait for you to meet each other."

"I'm looking forward to that myself. You know what? You sound sleepy." She felt his gaze on her face. "It's been a long day. Why don't you close your eyes for a little while?"

"Maybe just for a minute."

When next Catherine became aware of her surroundings, David was pulling into one of the guest parking slots near her condo entrance. It was dark.

Embarrassed to have fallen asleep, she cried, "I can't believe we're home already! After driving in that traffic, you're probably exhausted. If you'd rather look at the drawings another time, I'll understand."

"To be honest, I've been waiting for this moment all day. Much as I enjoyed watching the race, it was an excuse to be with you. Does that answer your question?"

She swallowed hard. "Yes." She didn't tell him she felt the same way.

She didn't have to.

CHAPTER FIVE

DAVID HADN'T SEEN the inside of her condo yet. When he'd arrived at seven that morning, Catherine had been waiting for him in the lobby.

All day, her thoughts had been focused on the time when they'd finally be alone together in the privacy of her living room. She was so physically aware of him, her fingers shook as she pushed in her code to gain entrance to the elevator. The ride to the second floor was accomplished in a matter of seconds.

"I have to admit I'm fascinated to see how an architect surrounds herself within the walls of her own home."

Unlocking the door, she smiled. "You're going to be surprised. I design for a contemporary world, but I think I was a provincial girl in another life."

She'd left a couple of lamps on.

"Incredible."

At the stunned tone of his voice, a warm feeling of satisfaction stole through her body.

His appreciative gaze traveled over the inlaid wood flooring to the far end of the room, where tall windows with transoms rose to the beamed ceiling.

Slowly he moved past the cherry wood kitchen

area to the chestnut dining table, touching the wood of one of the high-back Louis XV chairs with their rush inserts.

An old-world wrought-iron chandelier hung low. Beyond it, a massive eighteenth-century armoire stood against the stucco wall, its aged doors open to reveal a treasure of dishes in blue and yellow faience.

She watched him study the titles of books filling the ornate French étagères against another wall. After a moment, his attention switched to the flowered fabric on the carved wood couch; nearby stood a huge copper pot bursting with the same flowers.

"It feels like I just stepped inside one of those marvelous country villas tucked between fields of lavender and poppies somewhere in the south of France."

"Hardly a villa. But it's amazing what knocking out one wall can do."

He turned to her, his expression solemn. "No. It's much more than that. Your signature is everywhere. It illuminates everything you envision and touch, everything you wear. The way you smile."

While she reached for the portfolio propped against the sideboard in the kitchen, she tried to catch her breath. "Let's hope one of these drawings will appeal to you."

As she laid them out on the rectangular table so he could see each treatment, he closed the distance between them. "My only worry is that I'll want all of them. You might have to make the final choice for me.''

''Please don't give me that responsibility. Sit down and study them while I get us something to drink. What would you like? Tea? Coffee? A brandy?''

''Nothing for me, thank you. I have everything I want. Sit next to me.''

Trying to suppress her excitement, she joined him. Once they were seated, he reached for the closest drawing.

To present him with a variety of possibilities, she'd started with a spacious, all-white, four-story building, which exuded a light, contemporary feel. The next sketch featured a more traditional structure of steel and glass.

He said nothing, but his eyes went over every detail. Her heart pounded when he reached for the third drawing. Her favorite.

It showed a complex of buildings placed in their natural pine setting, with the added landscaping she'd envisioned. The other treatments were enlargements of the individual buildings, which showed the tall, beveled-glass windows to their greatest advantage. Each building was connected to the overall theme, using inlays of light and dark native woods against cedar.

He was quiet so long, she wondered if he was disappointed and didn't know how to tell her without hurting her feelings. Fearing the worst, she got up from the table and hurried into the kitchen to make a pot of tea.

"Remember," she called over her shoulder as she filled the kettle, "those are just preliminary sketches. If you haven't seen what you were hoping to find, I'll start again."

She was getting a box of tea bags from the cupboard when she heard a noise behind her.

"Don't you know I love them all?" His hands slid to her shoulders, caressing them with growing insistence. She felt his lips against her cheek. "But that's the least of my problems."

"W-what do you mean?" Her body was trembling.

He turned her in his arms, forcing her to look at him. "Are you going to pretend you don't know I've fallen in love with you?"

"David—"

"I don't care if it's too soon to tell you how I feel. When we met, something happened to me. Something profound. Earthshaking. In fact, during the last week, so much has gone on to transform my life, I'm still trying to comprehend it.

"Suffice it to say, I know the difference between fleeting attraction and this driving need to be with you every morning, every night and all the hours in between."

His eyes kindled a hot blue. "I want to stay, be with you—kiss you. But if you don't share my feelings, then tell me to leave and I'll get out of your life for good."

No—! You can't do that—not when I feel exactly the same way you do.

It was the truth.

She knew instinctively that this was the man she wanted to spend the rest of her life with. The man she wanted to father her babies.

Eight years ago, she'd felt an attraction for a man who'd turned out to be an opportunist and worse. She'd been naive, barely out of her teens. It had taken a long time to get over his betrayal, but she'd put the experience behind her, where it belonged. Since then she'd been careful.

Maybe too careful.

Now she was a woman with a woman's desires, and David Britton had blown into her life with the force of a tornado. In one meeting he'd turned all her preconceived notions upside down, uprooted her, carried her in new directions beyond her control.

If he hurt her, she would never get over it.

But if my fear of betrayal sends him away, I'll never be happy again.

She stared at him. "You know I don't want you to go."

No sooner had she whispered her confession than he lowered his mouth. She offered hers freely, needing to express everything she hadn't said in words.

"Catherine." Her name came out a smothered groan as he began giving her kiss after breathtaking kiss.

She held nothing back.

Each kiss grew longer, deeper. She forgot who

she was, where she was. Her only conscious thought was that she would die if this ecstasy came to an end.

"Tell me you love me." His voice sounded ragged as his lips caressed her throat.

"I thought that's what I was doing."

"I need to hear the words."

"What? That I'm so in love with you the ache never goes away?"

"Yes, those words," he murmured against her cheek. "I'm warning you now, I plan to marry you, and I'm not a patient man. Don't make me suffer too long."

"David, it's only been a week!"

"But I feel like I've known you all my life. It just took finding you."

"I know." She buried her face in his neck. "I feel the same way. It frightens me."

"How can anything this wonderful frighten you?"

"Because it's happened so fast and feels too perfect."

"Isn't this how real love is supposed to be? A rare collision in the cosmos between your universe and mine, joining us forever?"

Catherine would have said yes, but his lips were on hers again. She could deny him nothing. Slowly, inexorably, the heat of passion had her clinging to him.

"You know what?" he whispered in an unsteady

voice. "I want you too much right now. I'm going to leave while I still can."

Catherine groaned her protest.

"If you were a man, you'd understand. Go to bed. I'll pick you up at noon tomorrow, and we'll have a picnic out on the property."

"I'll fix it."

"Maybe next time." After an almost savage kiss, he made a decisive effort to put her away from him. "Don't walk me to the door. Otherwise I won't be responsible for the consequences."

She trembled with longing.

"Don't look at me that way, either," he whispered. "All I want you to do is bring the drawings tomorrow. I'd like to study them against the natural backdrop before I tell you which one I've selected."

"You haven't made up your mind yet?"

He smiled. "I know which one I want, and you do, too. It's simply another excuse to get you all to myself for as long as possible. You didn't have anything else planned for tomorrow, did you?"

"Only church, and that'll be over by eleven-thirty."

"Mind if I go with you?" He sounded as breathless as she felt.

"Mind?" she cried softly. "I wanted to ask you but didn't dare."

"What time do the services start?"

"At ten. It's about a mile from my condo."

"I'll come by for you at quarter to ten. Afterward,

we'll go back home and change into something casual, all right? When we've finished our picnic, I thought we'd take a long drive.''

''I can hardly wait. I'll be in the lobby.''

''Good night, Catherine.''

Feeling as if she'd been drugged, she locked the door after he'd gone, then prepared for bed. Her body was so on fire for him, she doubted she'd be able to close her eyes. But knowing that she'd see him in only a few hours provided a sense of contentment that finally calmed her, and she slept.

At nine-thirty the next morning, she was waiting for him in the lobby, already out of breath. To her joy, he arrived early, too. As soon as she saw his Mercedes, she emerged from the building with her portfolio and dashed toward him.

Smiling, he caught her in his arms. ''Do I dare hope this means you're excited to see me, or is the building on fire?''

She reciprocated with a full smile. ''To be completely honest, I'm so happy you're here, I can't think about anything else.''

They kissed hungrily. When he finally lifted his head, she noticed a solemn expression in his eyes. ''If it were all up to me, I'd head for Nevada and marry you before the day's over.''

He stowed her portfolio in the trunk. ''Let's hope your neighbors haven't called the police,'' he said with a grin. ''We're making a public spectacle of ourselves, as my mother might put it.''

"Any laws against that?" They both laughed as they pulled out of the drive into traffic.

That light moment seemed to set the tone for the whole day, which turned out to be gloriously warm and inviting. After an enjoyable church service, they both changed into jeans and T-shirts for their picnic, stopping first at her place, then at his. He filled a cooler and lugged it to his car.

He'd prepared thick ham sandwiches and pasta salad. There were hard-boiled eggs, fresh fruit and soft drinks. She ate too much, then groaned when he made her walk an imaginary path designating the foundation line for one of the buildings of his new complex.

She practically fell into his arms at the end. "I don't think I can do that again until this delicious meal digests."

"I don't want you to do it again. You were too far away from me." He cupped her face in his hands and started kissing her. Some teenagers driving by on the main road saw them and honked.

He relinquished her mouth before she was ready to let him go. "Come on, Catherine," he whispered. "Let's take that drive so we can be alone."

Together they gathered everything, including the drawings, and made their way to his car. For the rest of the day she marveled over the landscape as they wound their way through the Tillamook forest.

"Oh, David... Pull over to the side! Let's get out of the car for a minute." They'd crested a summit in the mountains, where they could look down a long straight, isolated road that went on for miles before disappearing into the lush vegetation. Both sides of the road were lined with row after row of trees—from the tiniest spring-green saplings to gigantic dark pines soaring into the blue canopy above. They towered to form an arch over the highway.

"It feels like we've just entered a cathedral," he said.

"But so much more glorious than anything manmade," she murmured, moved almost to tears by nature's beauty and the reverence in his voice. "Have you ever seen such a heavenly sight? Everything's perfect. Untouched. Smell the air. It's perfumed with a million Christmas trees!"

"Mmm." He put his arm around her shoulders and drew her against him. "Look at the different shades of green. Did you ever imagine there were so many?"

"No." She kissed his jaw. "I can count at least a dozen different species of pines all growing together. There must be dozens more we can't see from the car."

"Up on the mountain to your right, where the sun's rays have penetrated, the grass below those pines looks like green fire. Do you see it?"

"You're right!" She gasped in awe. "It's so beautiful, it seems unreal." She sighed in pure satisfaction. "What a perfect day this has been." She turned her head against his chest to look at him. "I'm happier than I've ever been in my life."

He drew in a deep breath. "What I'm feeling right now can't be expressed in words. All I can do is show you."

Last night he'd lit a fire when he kissed her. Ever since then, she'd been trying to keep it contained. But the second his mouth closed over hers, the fire exploded, sending out scorching flames that burned hotter and brighter. She couldn't get close enough to him.

"I'm in love with you, Catherine. I want you so badly I could carry you off beneath those trees and make love to you until long after the sun sets. When the air started to cool, I would hold you tight and keep you warm…until you begged me to make love to you again."

With David, it wasn't a case of begging him to do anything. *She* was the one who desired him to the last breath of her body. Her need for him was overpowering.

"You think I don't want that, too?"

"I know you do," he said softly. "But I'm also aware that you need more time. So I'm going to disentangle myself from your arms and get us out of here before I forget my good intentions."

He opened the passenger door and she got inside, not fastening her seat belt yet. As he settled himself in the driver's seat, he turned to her. She slid close to him and into the shelter of his right arm.

"From now on, you're going to have to set the pace. Now that I've found you, I've lost all self-control. Do you understand what I'm saying?"

"Yes."

"I ask only one thing."

"What's that?" Her heart wouldn't slow its erratic pounding.

"We have to see each other every day. I don't care if it's for five minutes." He made a fist on the steering wheel. "That's not true. Five minutes would never satisfy me."

"I couldn't stand that, either," she admitted, clinging to him as if he were saying goodbye to her for the last time. "I love you so much I'm afraid I can't focus on anything else."

Their mouths met once more in a lengthy kiss, a kiss that went on and on. Shadows of the evening darkened the interior before Catherine realized what she was inviting. He'd warned her it was up to her to set the boundaries.

Tearing her lips from his, she moved to the passenger side, and with trembling fingers, fastened her seat belt. Casting him a covert glance, she saw the way his chest heaved with emotion.

He placed his hand on her thigh as they started home in silence. It remained there, communicating his need. Helpless to do otherwise, she covered it with hers.

They were on fire for each other. She didn't care. David had become her whole world. She couldn't remember life before him.

"MR. BRITTON?"

"Yes, Louise?"

"May I see you for a minute, please?"

He'd barely walked into his office when his phone rang. But his secretary's tone suggested there was something that couldn't wait. "Of course," he said. "Just give me a minute."

Before he could get to his real work, he had to deal with the messages on his desk—urgent messages to call his mother, Mitch and his manager at the day trading office. They'd probably called him at home, too, but he hadn't even checked his voice mail last night. He closed his eyes, trying to summon his usual sense of purpose. It seemed his Monday morning was starting off with a series of problems.

All he could think about was Catherine.

They were going to have lunch together, but it wouldn't be for five hours. He might be able to last that long if he could hear her voice in the interim. As soon as he'd dealt with whatever business Louise was worried about, he'd phone Catherine at her office.

With that thought brightening his mood, he sat at his desk and waited for Louise

"You're here early this morning," he said when she appeared.

"I know." She shut the door, another sure sign of trouble. "Shannon White is outside in reception," she began in a quiet voice. "Barbara and I told her there were no job openings. She said that wasn't the reason she'd come."

David didn't believe that, but he kept his opinion

to himself. Whenever he was forced to think about Shannon, he experienced a feeling of distaste; with each incident, it was getting stronger.

"I reminded her that you couldn't see anyone without an appointment. That didn't matter to her. She said you'd make an exception as soon as you heard her news."

"What news?" he asked in a dull voice.

"She's found out that her twin is alive. An identical twin. A woman who's been spotted in downtown Portland."

He froze in his chair.

The thing he'd been hoping would never happen had come to pass.

So...today was payback time for the happiness he'd shared with Catherine yesterday. He should have known everything was too good to last. That was what she'd been saying all along. This latest bombshell proved how true that was.

He had no idea when or how Shannon had found out the truth, but that was irrelevant. She knew now, and wouldn't let it go.

"That's news, all right, provided it doesn't turn out to be a false lead," he said for Louise's benefit. "Thank you for alerting me. I'll tell you what. Let me have five minutes to get organized, then send her in.

"While you're at it, inform Ken that because of this interruption, I'll be starting the lab meeting ten minutes later than planned."

"Very good, Mr. Britton."

David understood his selfish reasons for hoping things would never get this far. But strictly speaking, the situation wasn't about him or his agenda.

No matter how he felt about Shannon, she had every right to pursue her lead. As the head of the Britton Institute, he would have to treat her as fairly as he would any other participant. Beyond that, he didn't have the right to give her information.

Catherine was the only person who could do that. But she didn't *know* she was a twin, otherwise that would have come out during his conversation with her on the drive home from Eugene. After what he'd learned, he could guarantee she wouldn't want to be found, even if she did know. It wasn't his place to tell Catherine anything, let alone persuade her one way or the other.

He heard a tap on the door. "David? Your secretary said it was all right to come in."

"Of course." As Shannon entered the room, he remained behind his desk to keep this meeting formal and brief. "I was just heading over to a staff meeting when Louise said you had some news that could be meaningful. I can spare a few minutes. Sit down," he said as she started toward him, her face and body radiating excitement.

His suggestion checked her movement. She found one of the chairs opposite his desk and perched on the edge of it.

After having been with Catherine all weekend, it was agony to face a euphoric Shannon and behave with any normalcy. He had to rate this moment as one of the most difficult of his life.

"Before anything else is said, Shannon, I want you to know that I recently learned of your interest in working for this institute. I'm sorry to have to tell you that despite your credentials, it's our policy not to hire anyone who's a participant. I was on the verge of asking Louise to send you a letter informing you of that."

"I understand. Oh, David—you're not going to believe what happened to me Friday night! I drove into Portland around seven and went to the same restaurant where you took me for dinner. That waiter, Steve, recognized me."

Forced to sit there without groaning, David listened while she explained how the impossible had happened.

Obviously, it *wasn't* impossible.

In fact, the more she talked, the more he knew in his gut that an eventual meeting of the twins would probably occur.

"I think the chances of this happening have to be in the billion-to-one category. You don't know what this means to me, how excited I am! She could easily have been a brother, but all along I've been hoping for a sister."

If this were anyone but Shannon, you'd tell her you're happy for her.

David nodded. "It sounds like a promising lead."

"I *know* it is!" she cried, her expression animated. "Whoever our mother is, she must have given birth in a hospital here in Oregon rather than Washington.

"As I told you before, after my adoptive mother died, I went through all her papers, but didn't find out anything about my adoption. If they had a birth certificate, I never saw it.

"When I checked birth records at the Washington State bureau of vital statistics, nothing turned up. Now I can check the Oregon records, as well. If I can find my twin, maybe her adoptive mother has more information about our births. I lay awake all night thinking about how wonderful it would be to find our birth parents, as well." She took a deep, shuddering breath. "David? I have a couple of ideas I want to run past you."

He feared what was coming next. "Go ahead."

"I've decided to hire a private investigator, but I also thought I'd take out a half-page ad in the Portland newspaper showing my picture. I'd offer a reward for added incentive. I could put something like, 'I'm looking for my identical twin sister. She recently had dinner at the Crompton Steakhouse. If you're that person, or if you know the name or address of the woman who looks exactly like me, phone me immedia—'"

"Wait a minute, Shannon," he broke in quietly. "Before you do anything, I want you to think seriously about what you're saying."

The eagerness left her face. "Why?"

"The institute was created for the genetic study of twins. In the whole time since its establishment, there have only been two sets of twins who happened to be united because they'd responded to our ads.

"Even though all four of them had been anxious to locate their twins, they found when they met that they had to go through a long, difficult period of adjustment."

Shannon shook her head. "I still don't understand what any of that has to do with me."

He sat back and folded his arms. "Think for a moment. Your mother's been gone a year. You've had twelve months to absorb the realization that you have a twin. All this time, you've been busy planning and anticipating a meeting. You answered our ad in the hope that it would lead you to him or her.

"Maybe you're ready for this monumental meeting, but your twin may not be. That's why you will have to tread carefully, however you go about tracking her down."

"What do you mean? When I heard I might have a twin, I could hardly wait to meet her!"

"Nevertheless, she may not feel the same way."

"But we're the same flesh and blood."

David patently didn't want Shannon to find Catherine, but he was required by law and his own code of ethics to give her the same advice he would give any participant who had come to him under these circumstances. It was vital that his conscience be free on this score, at least.

"Nevertheless you've lived apart for almost three decades, without the slightest knowledge of each other. A year ago, you learned you were adopted because your mother told you. But what if, for some reason, your birth parents couldn't afford both daughters, so they kept one and gave you up? What if they're all alive, yet never told their daughter she has a twin sister?

"Can you understand the damage that could be done to their family if your newspaper ad were to expose their secret in such a public way?

"The shock would be traumatic for all concerned. Trust would be lost and might never be regained. The daughter these parents loved might even run away. A divorce might result, because one of the parents had always wanted to tell their daughter the truth, and now it was too late to repair the damage. There are all kinds of devastating possibilities."

She lowered her head. "I guess I didn't think about it to that extent."

David felt he was making some progress. "Suppose your birth parents gave up both of you. What if your twin's adoptive parents never told her she was adopted, let alone that she was a twin?"

Her eyes flashed impatiently. "I can't imagine anyone doing that anymore. Not in this day and age."

"You'd be surprised. Some adoptive parents are afraid to tell the truth for fear they won't be loved as completely by their adopted children. Or they know the adoption was illegal and someone could get into trouble with the law if the news were to come out.

"Try to imagine how difficult it would be for them and their daughter to be approached by a private detective, or to see your picture in the paper. They could lose their daughter's love, the confidence of their friends, their employers, their neighbors. They might even end up in court."

He sat forward in his chair. "I learned a lot from the two sets of twins who found each other through my institute. Getting together with your sibling isn't just about you, Shannon. It's about whole families. In your case, you've lost your parents and you don't have brothers or sisters. For you it's much simpler. You've had time to think and prepare. You're open to a relationship."

"And you don't think she is."

At this point David was searching for words that wouldn't make him a complete liar. "Maybe she knows she's adopted. Maybe she knows she's a twin. But what if it doesn't mean anything to her? That's entirely possible. She may never have looked for her twin, never had any desire to meet him or her."

Shannon shook her head, "That's the part I can't believe."

"I understand that. But because she doesn't know you, she might not have your curiosity. Maybe she's happy with her life, maybe not. She could be married or single. She could be divorced. She could have children, or she might not.

"She might still be living at home taking care of an aged or sickly parent, like you were before your mother passed away. She might not want a twin in her life adding more complications.''

Taking advantage of her silence, he said, ''Then again, one day this woman might look for her twin, just the way you are. Maybe she's afraid to do an active search until her parents are gone, so it won't hurt them.

''Maybe she's always wanted to find her twin, and her adoptive parents have been helping her. Maybe she's married and her husband doesn't want her looking for a twin when she's needed at home, so she has to go about it in secret.

''Perhaps one day she'll see an ad like the one you responded to, and she'll contact the institute. The problem is that you assume finding your twin will make both of you happy. It could. It might. But there's a lot of hard work that goes on when you try to bond with a blood relative you've only just met.

''For what it's worth, I've talked at length with those twins who met through my facility. Along with their joy, they experienced pain and frustration. Even fear and anger. These emotions are bound to flare up when our lives are all so complicated, anyway.

''No matter how much you might want it, Shannon, you have to be prepared for the possibility that a bonding might never occur.''

He cleared his throat. ''I realize my words have dampened your excitement. But because of my position as head of this institute, I was compelled to say them.'' Everything he'd said was exactly what he would have told anyone in her circumstances. He *had* to issue these warnings, had to convey the complexity of such a situation. He'd tried to ignore the special knowledge he had in this case.

Shannon expelled a sigh. "I never expected this when I came here this morning. You've given me a lot to think about. I certainly wouldn't want to be responsible for hurting anyone."

In that moment David felt deeply sorry for her. He wished this whole situation were a nightmare that faded by morning.

"Having said all this, I have to tell you that, naturally, you're still free to do what you want." Should she ignore his advice and find a way to meet Catherine, anyway, he hoped she would do it with discretion.

He glanced at his watch and got to his feet. "I'm sorry, but I'm going to have to cut this short because I'm late for an important meeting."

Crossing the office, he opened the door for her.

Instead of walking past him, she stopped and put a hand on his arm. "David?" Her eyes held too much longing. Once again regret for past mistakes was torturing him. "I need to talk to you some more about this. Why don't I take you to dinner tonight?"

No more lies.

"Much as I appreciate the invitation, Shannon, I can't. I'm involved with someone else."

As she slowly let go of him, pain flickered across her face. "Is it serious?"

"Yes. Very."

Tears glazed her eyes. "So fast?"

Her bewilderment that he could have started seeing another woman this soon after their dinner date deepened his guilt. For her sake, he realized he had to be frank.

"Sometimes love happens like that," he said as gently as he could. "I'm planning to marry her."

She blinked.

David was halfway out the door before he thought of one more thing. "As I told you the first time, if your twin should ever come to this institute looking for her sibling, I'll call you immediately. That's a promise."

CHAPTER SIX

"Ms. Casey?"

"Yes, Janine?"

Her impressionable young secretary shut the door. "There's a *really* gorgeous guy out there to see you."

Catherine could think only of one man who fit that description, but they weren't planning to have lunch for at least two more hours.

She continued her drawing, but nothing seemed to be coming together. "I take it he doesn't have an appointment."

"He said he didn't need one." Janine walked over to the drafting table. "I'm supposed to give you this." She handed Catherine a small brown-paper bag.

Curious, she stopped what she was doing long enough to peer inside. Her pearls! The ones she'd worn to church yesterday. Her heart turned over, and she felt dizzy for a second.

"Send him in, Janine." She slid off her stool and hurried to the desk for her hairbrush.

"Shall I hold your calls?"

"Yes, please."

She'd just finished running the brush through her

hair when he appeared in the doorway with his po-
tent masculine presence.

"I know I'm early, but I couldn't keep away."

Catherine knew what he meant. It had been ludicrous to think she could get any work done, not
after the weekend they'd spent together. "Stay
where you are," she said in a shaky voice.

His beguiling smile melted her bones. "I don't
trust myself, either. There's something I want you
to see. It's about two blocks from here. We can grab
a bite along the way."

She couldn't imagine what made him sound so
excited, but it didn't matter. All she wanted was to
be with him.

"I'm coming."

She picked up her purse and followed him out of
her office, past Janine's desk, mouthing that she'd
be back soon. Her secretary happened to be on the
phone, but it didn't prevent her from staring at David as she smiled in understanding.

They hurried to the corridor. When the elevator
doors closed them inside, David pulled her into his
arms. "It's a good thing we're alone. I've got to do
this before I can think about anything else."

Catherine lifted her mouth to his, feverish for the
contact of his lips. They were still locked in an embrace when the doors opened on the main floor.

She reluctantly let go of him and turned to leave,
almost bumping into someone blocking the exit.

"Dad!"

While David stood there with enviable calm, still

holding her hand, she felt embarrassment scorch her cheeks.

"Hi, honey." Her father's eyebrows were raised. "If you're not too busy, how about introducing us?"

"Of course!" She stammered, feeling like an idiot. "Dad, I'd like you to meet David Britton. David, this is my wonderful, famous father, Cameron Casey."

Both men smiled and shook hands.

"Finally I'm understanding why my daughter seems to have disappeared from the face of the earth lately," her father said, blue eyes amused.

"Finally I get to meet *the* Casey," David murmured. "It's a real pleasure."

"I guess that means David was disappointed when he found out I was going to design his office complex instead of you, Dad."

Her father's keen gaze played over them. "From where I was standing, that's not how it looked."

She blushed again. "We're on our way to an early lunch. Would you like to join us?"

"I'd love to, but I've just come from breakfast and I'm late for an appointment. Why don't the two of you drive out to the house one night this week? Your mom's cold is better, and she told me she's missing you. Phone her later and set up a time."

"I will." She let go of David's hand to give her father a hug.

"You're glowing, honey. Must be someone special," he whispered against her cheek.

"He is," she whispered.

They waited until the elevator doors closed before David guided her out of the building to the sidewalk, where they started walking.

"Your father's a kind man, isn't he?"

It thrilled her David would discern that about him so quickly. "It's just one of his great qualities. He liked you, too."

"You think so?" He squeezed her hand a little tighter.

"Dad may be the nicest man on earth, but he's never issued one of my dates an invitation to the house on first meeting."

"Most likely that's because he's never caught you in a compromising position before, and he wants to find out if my intentions are honorable. Why don't we go in here?" he said, ushering her inside a small jewelry store advertising fine diamonds only. "Then he'll know they are."

A slight gasp escaped her throat. "David..."

Catherine's two closest girlfriends had been married for several years. She'd watched them fall in love, exclaimed over their engagement rings and cried at their weddings. Naturally she'd hoped it would happen to her, too. She just hadn't expected love to hit her this hard and fast when it did strike. Maybe she and David were so certain of their relationship because they were older. Perhaps their experience of life enabled them to recognize the depth of their feelings.

The jeweler placed a dozen unset diamonds of various cuts on a black velvet cloth in front of them.

David leaned close to her ear. "I know which one I'd like to see on your finger."

"So do I." She said it without hesitation, then smiled at him provocatively. "You guess."

His eyes searched hers, and she felt the force of his gaze through her entire body. "I don't think the designer in you would be happy with something conventional, so I'm going to choose the pear shape."

She shouldn't have been surprised, not when he was so in tune with her feelings. The corner of his mouth lifted in a half-smile. "I'm right, aren't I?"

"You know you are," she answered in a husky voice.

Despite the jeweler looking on, he brushed his lips against hers. "That was easy."

After they'd chosen a mounting and the jeweler sized the ring, David said, "Shall we go to that crêpe restaurant we passed? Or will you fly with me to a private island for the rest of the week? The decision is yours."

"I wonder what you'd do if I asked you to drive us to the airport."

His eyes narrowed on her mouth, taking her breath away. "Ask, and find out."

She felt a surge of excitement that left her physically weak. "Don't tempt me, David. Maybe we'd better eat. Then I have to get back and pretend to do some work at the office before I leave for the site today.''

''Unfortunately I have commitments, too. But tonight we'll be together for the symphony. I'll come by for you at seven. That reminds me—we've been invited to dinner tomorrow night at the Hales'. Allen's wife said it's casual.''

''Is he a friend you met through business?''

''No.'' He kissed her mouth once more. ''A great buddy from my high school days. We've remained close. He and his wife can't wait to meet the woman I'm going to marry.''

WHEN A FAMILY was ready to put an ailing member in a nursing home, the ordeal drained everyone. A big part of Shannon's job was to provide reassurance. But this was Thursday night, and she'd put in a grueling four days since returning from Portland.

''My husband's been getting progressively worse,'' the elderly woman said in a tearful voice. ''Now that he's incontinent, I can't take care of him anymore.''

Shannon eyed her with compassion. ''Of course not. He'll get excellent care here, Mrs. Stevens. It won't be the way you do things, but we'll make sure he's comfortable. Ralph is a strong man and a good nurse. He'll be able to assist your husband and give him a massage every day.''

''Even if my husband doesn't know me, I plan to come in most days to help him eat his dinner. My son will drive me.''

"How fortunate for you. I'm glad you have your son's support. And I'm sure anything you can do for your husband will make him happy, and it'll also make you feel better. So I'll see both of you in the morning somewhere between ten and twelve. Remember to bring all his medications. The doctor will want to discuss everything with you then."

"Yes, Ms. White. Thank you."

Shannon took the woman's arm and walked her to the large lobby of the nursing home. Considering its function, it was a beautifully designed and furnished place. Before she died, Shannon's mother had learned to like it.

"Good night," she called after Mrs. Stevens.

Anxious to leave work and go to her friend Amy's for a heart-to-heart, she hurried to her office to lock up.

"Hello, Shannon."

She whirled around in surprise because she didn't know anyone had come in. "Steve!"

The waiter from the steakhouse got up from the chair by her desk. He was dressed in a T-shirt and jeans instead of his uniform, and she realized he was an attractive man.

"Do you have news for me?" she asked excitedly. "Did you do something illegal for me, after all?"

He cocked his head while he studied her features and uniformed figure. "Does a guy have to have a reason to come and see you?"

Her spirits plummeted. "No. But it's quite a drive from Portland to Tacoma just to say hello."

"Not if a guy's interested. The first time you came to the restaurant, you were with a date. The second time you came alone. Since you weren't wearing a ring either time, I thought I'd take my chances and see if you'd like to go out with me."

"I don't know you."

He smiled. "That's why I'm here. My name is Steve Jarvis, and I'm working my way through graduate school waiting tables. How about going for a drink somewhere? Or would I be, shall we say, trespassing on private property?"

Much as I appreciate the invitation, Shannon, I can't. I'm involved with someone else.... I'm planning to marry her.

"No. You wouldn't be doing that, but tonight isn't a good time. I'm sorry."

His expression sobered. "So am I." He reached in his pocket. "Before I leave, you might want this." He handed her a folded piece of paper. "I did something I shouldn't. Please don't get me in trouble. It's the name and address of the guy who was with your twin."

She was incredulous. "You did that for me?"

"Yeah. Well, you did pay me. Of course, I wish I could have given it to you while we were having a drink, but you win a few and you lose a few." He backed away. "Good luck meeting up with her."

"Thank you," she finally murmured, still in shock. But she ended up saying it to an empty room.

Fifteen minutes later, she arrived at Amy's apartment.

"Look!" Shannon said without preamble.

Amy took the paper from her. "Jack Casey, 3901 Blue Spruce Drive, Portland, Oregon." She darted Shannon a glance. "What does this mean?"

"This is the man who was with my twin at the steakhouse. That waiter, Steve, just brought it to me."

"He *brought* it to you? All the way from Portland? My, my."

"I paid him, remember?"

"That's true. But, Shannon—this means you've found her!" Amy threw both arms around her.

"Yes!"

"My only problem is approaching this Jack without getting Steve in trouble. He took the information off a copy of the credit card receipt."

"That's easy. Just tell the guy you asked the waiter for his help in finding your sister, and he thought he remembered the name Casey from when he ran the credit card through. With that much information, you finally tracked him down on your own."

Shannon nodded. "I think that could work."

"Of course it will."

"I'm going to see if Laurie will cover for me tomorrow so I can drive to Portland in the morning."

Amy frowned. "After what David Britton said to

you, maybe it'd be better if you got this guy's number through information and phoned him first."

She might not want a twin in her life adding more complications. "You're right. I'm being too impatient."

"No one could blame you. Why don't you call him right now?"

Needing no encouragement, Shannon called information, but the number was unlisted by request. There was another number for a Cameron Casey at the same address. Would she like that?

Shannon quickly wrote it down.

Amy hovered nearby. "Did you get it?"

"It's for a Cameron, not Jack, but they're both at the same address."

"Hmm. Do you want me to call and ask for Jack? If he's there, I'll give you the phone."

"No, because I'm not supposed to know his first name, remember?"

"That's right! Then I'll call and say I'm looking for a man with the last name of Casey who had dinner at the steakhouse in Portland recently. If either one of them is that person, I'll ask him to call me back collect. How does that sound?"

After thinking about it, Shannon couldn't find anything wrong with the plan. "They'll probably think we've found something of theirs and want to return it. That's good. Go ahead and try."

She held her breath while her friend made the call. It didn't take very long. Amy put down the receiver. "The man who answered said he'd never eaten at the steakhouse but he couldn't answer for his son, so he'd give him the message.''

"So Jack is his son. Well, I guess it's a waiting game now.''

"I'll order a pizza while you find us a video.''

WITH MELANIE WORKING LATE at her job at the Red Cross blood bank, Jack let himself in the door of his apartment at the back of his parents' house, anxious to study the video from last Saturday's race.

He'd seen it before, but other people were around. Now that he was alone, he wanted to watch it again. He had a couple of hours before he needed to pick up Melanie, and this time he would figure out where he'd gone wrong.

Out of the corner of his eye he saw a note in his dad's handwriting. It had been slipped under the door.

Call Amy Walsh collect if you've recently had dinner at the new steakhouse in Portland. 253-555-9871.

It was a Tacoma, Washington, area code.

He tried to remember if he'd left something behind at the restaurant. Or maybe his credit card hadn't gone through. That didn't seem likely since he'd paid off most of it. Still…

He decided he'd better call and find out what they wanted before he started watching the video.

He reached for his cell phone and punched in the number, not bothering with the suggestion that he call collect.

"This is Jack Casey. I'm returning your call."

"Just a minute, please."

While he waited, he fast-forwarded the video to the middle of the race, where he'd started to fall behind.

"Hello? Mr. Casey?"

"Yes."

"Are you the Casey who had dinner at the steakhouse in Portland a few weeks ago?"

"That's why I'm returning your call. Who is this?"

"I—I don't want to say or do anything wrong. Before I answer that question, would you please be gracious enough to answer one other question for me?"

The woman's voice, the hesitation, sounded oddly familiar. A strange sensation traveled up his spine.

He forgot about the video. "Go ahead and ask."

Another hesitation. "The blond woman you were with that night—is she a friend or a relative?"

He blinked. *It was Shannon.* He'd known it in his gut when he first heard her speak.

He thought back to the night he and Catherine had eaten dinner at the steakhouse and remembered how all that business about her double had come up. The waiter was the only person who would have seen Jack's full name printed on the credit card. That was the only possible way this woman could have made a connection.

"You're Shannon, aren't you?"

There was a silence. "Shannon White," she finally said. "Amy Walsh is a friend of mine. I'm at her place."

"I think you and I had better meet."

"Thank you." Heartfelt emotion was conveyed in those words. "When?"

"I'll get back to you. It may be a while."

"I understand. You're very kind. Thank you."

"You're welcome."

He clicked off.

The sweetness in her voice, the vulnerability—it was Catherine all over again. Those very qualities had always made him want to protect his sister. There was no question in Jack's mind that he'd just spoken to Catherine's identical twin.

David Britton had some explaining to do.

IT WAS SUNDAY. The long-awaited day of the family council. David pulled into the driveway of his mother's two-story colonial house behind Mitch's Jeep. He was ten minutes late.

After attending church with Catherine, David had gone to her place. They'd planned to fix breakfast. But they only made it as far as pouring juice before they fell into each other's arms. From then on, he'd lost track of time.

If Catherine's mother hadn't phoned, asking her to bring him to the house for dinner that night, David would have forgotten about the meeting at his mother's.

Catherine understood he had to leave, but she'd clung to him for a long moment. It was harder and harder to be apart, for any reason. He had a solution, though, and was glad he'd be meeting her mother.

Next week, he planned to introduce Catherine to his mother. The sooner both families realized how things were between him and Catherine, the sooner they could set a wedding date.

With a promise that he'd be by later to drive her to her parents' home, he left for his mother's. His body was still throbbing from a desire he could barely hold in check.

Mitch, who must have been watching for him through the living room window, met him at the front door.

"You're late. Mom's putting lunch on the table already."

"Sorry, but I couldn't get here any sooner."

A knowing smile broke out on Mitch's face. "I've never seen you like this in my life. Whatever Catherine's done to you, you're a mess."

"It'll happen to you, too—when you least expect it."

"Have you told Mother yet?"

"I will before lunch is over."

They walked through the house to the dining room where their mother was bringing in a salad and a platter of ham. She might be in her late sixties, but she had the figure of a younger woman and kept her hair a natural brown color to hide the gray.

How sad their father wasn't still alive. Since Catherine had come into David's life, he couldn't imagine existence without her. No wonder his mother's grief had been so acute.

"Let me help you with that."

"Oh—David! You're here. I'm so glad. Everyone sit down. Mitch, dear? Will you say the blessing, please?"

"I'd be happy to."

Since their visit to the psychiatrist, David could see a difference in Mitch. He didn't act as wary or defensive.

"Thank you, Mitch. Now if you'll start passing the ham and scalloped potatoes. David, if you'd toss the salad." Soon everyone was served, and they began to eat.

"This is my favorite meal of yours, Mother. Would you mind if I asked you to fix it again next Sunday?"

"Of course I wouldn't mind. But why?"

"Because I'd like to bring someone home for dinner."

"A business acquaintance?"

"No. The woman I'm going to marry."

His mother let out a cry of joy and rushed around the table to hug him. "That's the most wonderful news I've heard in a long, long time!"

He stood and hugged her. "Her name is Catherine Casey. She lives here in Portland. Her father is Cameron Casey, the architect. You may have heard of him. She's an architect, too. In fact, I've hired her to design my new complex. We're not officially engaged yet, but we've picked out her ring.

"I've even seen a piece of property where I'd like us to build our home. I've already contacted my attorney to make an earnest money offer."

"That's wonderful!" She wiped her eyes. "Have you met her yet, Mitch?"

"Yes. Last week David brought her to the track. She's a gorgeous blonde with gray eyes and a knockout figure. I wish *I'd* seen her first."

"Sit down, Mother, and I'll answer all your questions."

"This is so exciting, David!" she said after she'd taken her place once more. "When do you plan to be married?"

"I'd arrange for a minister today, but Catherine needs more time. We only met two weeks ago."

"Two weeks! Well, of course she needs more time!"

"I'm hoping for a fall wedding. Preferably September. That gives us two months to plan. We talk constantly about everything, and I feel I know her in a way I've never known a woman before. We agree on everything that's important." He paused. "I'm not getting any younger, and she'll be twenty-nine on her next birthday. We've decided that once we're married, we don't want to put off having children."

"A grandchild—"

The happiness in her voice let David know this revelation had lifted her spirits immeasurably.

"I have some news, too, Mother."

David eyed his brother, wondering what was coming.

"If it's about your racing, I really don't want to talk about it."

"I've given it up."

She pushed her chair away from the table and started clearing dishes. "So you can do something even more dangerous—like skydiving?" Her retort was sharp.

"No, Mother. Please—sit down. I'm trying to tell you something. If you'll hear me out, you won't need to run into the kitchen to take your headache medicine."

"That was very unkind of you, Mitch."

"I didn't mean it to be. Please. I want to talk to you."

Slowly she took her place again, but her expression remained haunted.

"This fall I'm going to start graduate school and work on getting my MBA."

"*What?*"

"Dad ran a very successful insurance agency. David built his own day trading company. I figure it's time I found out what I'm going to do with the rest of my life. I need to rely on myself and become independent, too."

Their mother hurried around the table and broke down sobbing in Mitch's arms.

David struggled to hold back tears. That must have been some conversation the doctor had held with Mitch. Obviously, it was as illuminating as his talk with David.

"Before my school starts, I thought maybe the three of us could take a week off and go up to Banff and Lake Louise, like we used to do when Dad was alive. I can't remember the last time we vacationed together. We could leave in a few days and on the way back, we could drive through Glacier Park. What do you say?"

Sobbing with happiness, their mother couldn't speak.

David smiled at his brother over her head. Much as he didn't want to leave Catherine, he knew this vacation was vital for their mother's mental health. While they were away, they'd be able to talk about past guilt. It could be a healing time for everyone.

A week apart from Catherine would be agony. But David had a gut feeling it would work in his favor. Before he'd left her condo, she'd admitted that she wished they were already married. Once he returned from his trip, she'd be ready to set the date.

"It sounds like a terrific idea, Mitch. I'll talk to my secretary in the morning and clear my calendar."

Their mother lifted her head and smiled. "I'm so happy," she whispered, "I can hardly stand it."

David and Mitch exchanged a triumphant grin.

WHILE HER DAD showed David around the spacious, modern house he'd designed years earlier, Catherine followed her mother to the kitchen, ostensibly to help her dish up dessert.

Shorter than her daughter, with brown eyes and red hair she often wore in a ponytail, Robyn Casey had a vivacious and charming personality. Catherine could tell David felt at home with her parents, as if he'd known them for years.

"Where's Jack, Mom? I thought he'd be here for dinner."

"I really don't know. He said he had something important to do, and we should expect him and Melanie when we saw them."

"Did he realize you'd invited David?"

"Yes. Apparently he couldn't get out of a prior commitment. Is something wrong?" She took out a homemade chocolate pie from the refrigerator.

"Oh, no. I just hoped they'd be here."

"I'm sure he'll come as soon as he can. Your brother knows you've fallen in love. He wouldn't miss this without a good reason. Just yesterday, he said he was afraid you'd make it to the altar before he did."

Catherine blinked. "But I haven't mentioned mar—"

"You didn't have to," her mother interrupted with a smile. "When your father got home from the office the other day, he said he'd never seen two people so absolutely crazy about each other. After watching you tonight, I agree. What's so nice is that I've fallen for him myself. Heavens, what's not to like?"

"Nothing," Catherine agreed, beaming.

"Besides so many attractive qualities, David has accomplished some truly remarkable things for a man of any age, let alone one who's still in his thirties! Let's face it. You're my only daughter, and I expect near perfection from the man you choose. If I had to pick out a son-in-law, I would say David Britton comes closest to my ideal for you. He accepts everything about you, but challenges you, too. I think you've met your match."

"I'm so glad you feel that way! He's wonderful, Mom. I love him so much. He wants to get married soon, but I'm nervous because it's happened so fast."

"Falling in love *is* scary. There are no guarantees. The first time I met your father, I knew he was the man I was going to marry. On the surface he was very funny. Clever and charming. But there was a strength in him that I sensed right away. It told me he was the one. Sound familiar?"

"Oh, yes."

"We got married fast. It might not have lasted. Many marriages don't. We were very lucky, and we worked very hard at it.

"If David's the one, and it appears that he is, you'll know when it's right to set a date. Just remember that he's waited a lot longer than you have to find his soul mate. Now that you've come along, naturally he's eager."

She finished cutting the pie and put liberal slices on plates. "Shall we take these into the lounge for

David and your father? I've already got coffee out there.''

With a few remarks, her mother had managed to put everything into perspective for Catherine. Her words had driven out the last lingering doubts caused by that damaging love affair in college.

Catherine threw her arms around her mother. ''Thanks, Mom. I needed this tonight.''

''So did I. I've been waiting a long time to see the stars in your eyes. It's a sight every mother longs for,'' she said softly. ''Now, come on. Let's go feed those hungry men.''

When they reached the lounge, David and her father were deep in discussion. But the second they saw Catherine and her mother, they got up to take the plates and put them on the coffee table.

''I've just learned that David's brother, Mitch, has been in some of the same races as Jack,'' her father announced. ''You two have more in common than I thought.''

David sent Catherine a private glance. ''Except that it was never his *raison d'être* the way it is with Jack. In fact, while I was with my family earlier today, he told us he's giving it up for good to go to graduate school. His decision has given my mother a new lease on life.''

''We know exactly how she feels, don't we, darling?'' Catherine's mother grasped her father's hand.

''But it's even been harder on David's mother, who's a widow.'' Catherine launched into an explanation of the SIDS tragedy that had robbed the Britton family of one of its sons and left his mother riddled with guilt.

"That's why David initially created the twin studies institute. To try to help her understand that his death wasn't her fault."

David had told Catherine about his feelings of guilt over the stuffed toy, and the reason Mitch's survivor guilt had forced him to stare death in the face. But those revelations were private.

"I envy you, David," Robyn confessed. "You no longer have to worry about Mitch the way we fear for Jack's life every time he gets behind the wheel of his race car."

"Did I just hear my name taken in vain?"

CHAPTER SEVEN

"HI, EVERYBODY. Sorry we're late. Melanie's family had company at their house, too. We got away as soon as we could." Jack's gaze met David's. He gave him a nod. "Good to see you."

"Thank you. It's wonderful to have been invited," David replied. He caught Catherine's hand closer to him.

Jack had greeted him in a normal, friendly manner. Yet, somehow, David sensed that something was wrong.

"We're thrilled you made it," Catherine's mother said. "Do you two want some pie?"

Melanie shook her head. "Thank you, but I don't think I could."

"What about you, Jack?"

"Save a piece for me, and I'll eat it later. We just had strawberry shortcake at her house."

Catherine's father smiled at him. "While you were eating poor Melanie's family out of house and home, we found out you're going to be minus one competitor from now on. David tells us his brother has put his race car away to go back to school."

Jack's eyebrows shot up. "That *is* news. Tell me more about it while we go out to the garage for a minute, David. There's something I want to show you."

I knew it.

"Oh, no—no guy things tonight," Catherine moaned. "Once you get out there, you'll never come back."

Jack grinned. "I promise this won't take long."

"We'll time you," Melanie said with a chuckle. "If you're not back in twenty minutes, Catherine and I will come looking for you."

David's glance swerved to Catherine's. "Promise you'll rescue me?" he murmured for her ears alone. She nodded, smiling, and the love light in her eyes almost blinded him. "I'll hurry," he whispered, then kissed her cheek and got up from the sofa.

He and Catherine's brother left the house and headed for the garage down the drive. "Has Mitch really given up racing?" Jack asked him.

"Yes, much to my mother's relief. He was never involved in it for the same reason you are. Right now, he wants to focus on getting his MBA."

"You don't think he'll regret it one day?"

"Never. It's not in his blood. You're the one who's truly passionate about it. You know, I meant what I said last week. You keep driving the way you are and you'll make it to the top."

"Thanks, David." Jack unlocked the door to the garage and turned on the lights. David followed him inside and shut it behind them.

"I can tell there's something important on your mind."

"So you knew I got you out here for a reason."

"Let's just say I had a feeling."

"Okay. Here goes. I got a phone call from a woman on Thursday night. Somehow, she'd learned that I was the Casey who had dinner at the steakhouse with a blond woman several weeks ago. She wanted to know if this woman was a friend or a relative. I didn't tell her anything, but I promised I'd call her back. After talking it over with Melanie, I decided to come to you first."

Jack put his hands on his hips. "Just answer me one question. When CC bumped into you at the track, how come you didn't tell her right then that Shannon was her identical twin sister?"

Somehow, before Jack had even opened his mouth, David had known this had everything to do with Shannon. He looked Catherine's brother in the eye. "It may be a simple question," he began. "But there's no simple answer. In essence, this is the situation."

Jack listened intently while David filled him in. "I had hoped this day would never come," David admitted. "But now that it has, I'm going to have to break institute rules and tell Catherine the truth. I don't want Shannon getting to her first.

"I'm in love with your sister and I plan to marry her. I've tried to protect her as long as I could, but I hadn't counted on that waiter's interference."

"Oh, man— What a hell of a mess." Jack eyed him with compassion. "CC's going to go into shock to find out she's a twin. I'm sure the folks have no idea.''

David took a fortifying breath. "Let's put off phoning Shannon until Catherine's had a chance to deal with her feelings." Jack nodded. "If Catherine doesn't want to meet her, then I'll tell Shannon the truth and she'll have to accept it. You don't need to get any more involved. Shall we go back? They're going to wonder where we are."

They left the garage and started up the drive. "You're a good man, David. I couldn't want better for my sister."

"Thanks, Jack," he murmured. "It means a lot that you came to me first. I admire that more than you know."

No sooner did they step inside the living room than Catherine hurried over to greet him. "I was just about to come and get you."

He slid his arm around her shoulders. "Let's go home."

Catherine turned to her family. "David and I have to be at work early in the morning. Much as we hate to leave, we're going to have to. Thank you for the delicious dinner. We had wonderful time. It's great to see you, Melanie."

David shook her father's hand and gave her mother a hug. "I second everything Catherine said. This has been a delightful evening. I've been anxious to meet both of you. As for Jack and Melanie, we'll look forward to seeing you at the next race."

Her parents followed them through the house to

the front door, where good-nights were exchanged. Within minutes David was behind the wheel, ready to drive them to the city.

Before he started the engine, he leaned across the seat for a swift kiss. "You have a terrific family, Catherine. I don't know when I've enjoyed an evening more." He set off down the long drive.

"Mom and Dad enjoyed it, too. They were very impressed with you."

He smiled at her. She reached for his hand and lifted it to her lips.

"I love you, Catherine. You've become my whole life. I hope you know that." He paused, taking a deep breath. "Something has come up to do with my work, and you need to be told about it."

He felt her eyes on him. "Are you talking about the day trading company or the institute?"

"The latter. As you know, we compile data on identical twins to study their genetic differences and similarities. The research scientists in the lab are finding out that some effects attributed to environment may actually be due to subtle genetic and other biological differences between supposedly identical twins.

"In order to make predictions, they need thousands of subjects to study. Every day more twins around the country answer our ads, providing us with the information we need.

"But there's another aspect to this. We also put out ads to attract people who think they *might* be twins."

She stirred in her seat. "What do you mean, think?"

"Have you ever known a pair of identical twins?"

"No."

"Having grown up with Mitch, I noticed that he exhibited certain characteristic signs of wanting and needing another person to make him feel complete. It was almost as if he sensed he'd lost a part of himself and was trying to find it. No matter what Mother or I did for him, it was never enough.

"As a child, when he made friends with other kids, he wanted more than they were willing to give. He had almost a need to possess them. This intense desire to share a special closeness alienated his friends, so he turned to hobbies.

"Until the data started to come in, I didn't understand Mitch's behavior the way I do now. He's not so different from other twins who've lost their siblings and can't find comfort.

"It's not a conscious thing and has more to do with psychic experiences that transcend those of non-twin siblings. Scientists refer to the phenomenon as a psychic bond in which twins share thoughts and feelings even though they might live thousands of miles from each other.

"Obviously, something we don't understand goes on in the womb. Twins are born with a feeling of connection. Without it, they're like wanderers. Not all of them, of course. And certainly those needs vary widely in degree.

"I hope that, one day, someone will come along who relates to Mitch on that special level and fills the void. If it's anything like the way you and I communicate, he'll be a lucky man.

"But to get back to my point, some people write or phone the institute telling us they've had experiences that led them to believe they've got a twin somewhere, even though there's no real proof.

"Occasionally, we hear from people who've learned from a certain source, reliable or otherwise, that they have a twin but were separated at birth or in the formative years. This starts them on a search.

"The institute keeps records on all of these people. Once in a while, a pair of twins contacts us without either one being aware of it. They've both been dedicated to finding their sibling. When we receive the data and realize through DNA testing that it's a match, we can be the catalyst to bring them together."

"Does this happen very often?"

"Twice so far."

"That's extraordinary! Were they happy to have found each other?"

"Very happy. But consider for a moment how people might feel if they had no idea they were a twin and then were confronted by their long-lost sibling."

She shook her head. "It would be such a shock, I can't even imagine it. Of course, knowing how much Jack wants to find his birth parents, I suspect he'd love it. I can see him now. If he discovered he had a twin, he—"

Suddenly she stopped talking. He could practically hear her thinking.

"David? I can tell you've been leading up to something," she said slowly. "Are you saying Jack has an identical twin who's been looking for him?"

He pulled into a guest parking spot at her building. "I wish I could say yes to your question."

Catherine had been so certain she was right, it took a minute for David's words to sink in. When they did, she realized this had nothing to do with Jack.

Her mind flashed to that moment at the speedway.

I think maybe it's time you and I had a little talk, Shannon.

She remembered the waiter's words.

You don't happen to have an identical twin sister, do you?

"*I'm* the one with the twin sister, aren't I?"

His sharp intake of breath resounded in the car. "Yes. Shannon came to the institute over a month ago to participate in the study. I sometimes do the initial interview. As it happened, I asked her out and wrote down the information during dinner. She said her mother had told her she was a twin, so she's been looking for her sibling.

"Ever since that waiter, Steve, told her she had a double, she's asked him to keep an eye out for you. When he remembered Jack's name, he told her. That's when she phoned Jack."

"Now I understand why he wanted to talk to you in the garage!"

"Yes."

"Did Jack tell this Shannon about me?"

"No. He said nothing for the same reason that I didn't tell her I met you at the track. I didn't have the legal or moral right to divulge something to you when you're not a participant at the institute."

He shook his head. "Jack came to me because he knows it's only a matter of time before she tracks you down. I knew you had no interest in your birth family, so I kept it from you, thinking you'd never have to know."

Shock didn't begin to describe what Catherine was feeling. But somehow David understood. In the next instant, he'd crushed her in his arms.

"Catherine, there was no easy way to tell you. Please forgive me."

"What's there to forgive?" she cried, clinging tightly. "If anything, I hope you can forgive me."

"For *what?*"

"For being an awful person," she whispered. "At the moment, I don't like myself very much. It's embarrassing to have to admit that to you, of all people."

"Why do you say that?"

"Because tonight you gave me some information that would seem terribly exciting to anyone else. But that's not how I feel. My life's been wonderful for twenty-eight years, and getting more wonderful all the time."

"I know."

"I want everything to stay just as it is. I don't want to know anything about her. I've never had any sense of being a twin, of missing something. Her life has never had anything to do with mine. I can't help that I don't feel the way she does. The fact is, we've lived apart all these years. I have no desire to meet her, David. No interest at all."

"Then you don't have to, and we'll never discuss it again."

"You mean it?"

"Catherine, what I told you places you under no obligation. The institute wasn't created for the purpose of uniting two people who never knew about each other.

"Shannon believed she had a twin and responded to our ad. But I told her at the beginning that unless her twin contacted the institute for the very same reason, a reunion couldn't possibly happen.

"Even though we live only a few blocks apart, the odds of my meeting you accidentally were pretty incredible."

"Yes. I still can't believe it."

"Neither could I, at the time. And, like a physician, I was bound to a code of silence in this very delicate situation."

Catherine nodded.

"When you asked me if you reminded me of Shannon, I was forced to reveal that the two of you bore a superficial resemblance to each other. You seemed satisfied with my answer. That was as much as I dared tell you. But the waiter's actions have changed everything.''

''I realize that.''

''I'll call Shannon and let her know you're not interested in a meeting. She'll have to accept that as final.''

He got out of the car and escorted her into the building. She unlocked the door and didn't understand why he didn't walk inside with her. ''David?''

''The way I'm feeling about you tonight, if I come in, I won't leave at all.'' He pulled her into his arms. ''Catherine, there's something else I need to tell you. I've been putting it off. Today at Mother's we made a decision to take a family vacation in Banff, our first since before my father's death. Mother needs a change.

''Mitch phoned me on my way to your condo. He said she wants to leave right away, tomorrow if possible.''

Catherine groaned.

''This is progress for her. We have to do it, for her sake. I'll probably be home next Saturday night.''

David was going away for a week?

''I'm afraid I'll miss your brother's race here in Portland on Saturday, but we could plan to attend the one in Vancouver the week after. You're invited to my mother's for dinner a week from today. She can't wait to meet you.''

''I'm looking forward to meeting her, too,'' Catherine whispered.

A hand lifted her chin. "Don't you know I dreaded telling you this? The thought of spending any time away from you is killing me! I'll be calling you so often, you won't get any work done."

"Ever since I met you, I haven't been able to concentrate on anything but you."

"Me, too. My secretary, Louise, is ready to fire me."

She closed her eyes. "How am I going to let you go?"

"If we hadn't had this breakthrough with Mother—"

"I know," she cried softly. "I'm being selfish. It's because I love you so much."

"Keep telling me that. I can't hear it enough."

On a shaky breath, she said, "When you get back, let's set a date."

"Catherine…"

THE STEAK RESTAURANT in the Crompton warehouse didn't start serving dinner until five o'clock.

Shannon stood in line outside, waiting for it to open. Apparently, Wednesday brought in as many patrons as Friday night did.

She was too far away to peer through the glass. Was Steve there this evening? If he didn't work the Wednesday-night shift, then Shannon was wasting her time. Knowing how busy the waiters were, she'd decided against phoning the restaurant. The only thing to do was talk to him in person. If he wasn't here, she'd find out his schedule and come back another time.

To her relief the doors finally opened. She shuffled behind the others until the hostess greeted her.

"How many are in your party?"

"One. Could you tell me if Steve is working tonight? He's a very good waiter. I'd like to be served by him again if I could."

"Wait just a minute and I'll find out if he's on." Soon the hostess reappeared. "Yes. He's here. I'll take you to one of his tables."

Shannon followed her to a corner spot. "He'll be right with you," the woman said, then handed her a menu and left. For want of anything else to do, she studied it.

"Hello."

She lifted her head and saw pleasure on Steve's face.

"Hello. I'm glad you're on duty tonight because I came expressly to see you."

"Does that mean you're not going to eat again?"

"No. I'll have the same thing I had the first time."

His eyes danced. "Steak. Medium rare."

"That's right. Steve, do you get a break in the next little while?"

"Sure. I'll put in your order. When it's ready, I'll bring it out and sit with you for a few minutes. Brad can cover for me that long."

"Thank you."

Steve must have rushed her meal, because he was

back in less than twenty minutes. He served her, then drew up a chair.

"I needed to thank you in person," Shannon began. "Not only for driving all the way to Tacoma, but for going out on a limb for me. I was as discreet as possible. I told the man in question that I asked you if you remembered anything, and that you thought the last name was Casey. I tried very hard to make sure you wouldn't get in trouble."

He folded his arms, eyeing her steadily. "I believe you. Now, are *you* going to go out on a limb and accept a date with me? I want to hear about this quest for your twin, but right now's not a good time."

She hesitated. "How old are you?"

"Twenty-four."

"Just as I thought. I'm twenty-eight, going on twenty-nine. I only date older men."

"I'm going on twenty-five," he said. "Hey, that makes me older."

Shannon had to admit she'd never met a younger man as self-assured as he was. He was good-looking, too; Amy would say he was really cute with those dimples and that black wavy hair.

"I'll have to think about it." She took a bite of salad. "Before you go back to work, can I ask you an important question?"

"Sure."

"If it was my twin you were talking to right now, would you be just as interested in taking her out?"

A frown appeared on his face. "Hell, no! Are you

accusing me of being some kind of womanizer or something?''

"Of course not," she tried to assure him, surprised by his reaction. "But you said we were identical."

"You are, physically. But in talking to you, I can tell you're as different as night and day."

"Really? You can tell that just by taking our orders?"

"You'd be surprised what you can learn about people from waiting on them." His mouth curved in a slow smile. "If she'd been the woman I was attracted to, I would have called Jack Cascy myself. I sure as hell wouldn't have driven all the way to Tacoma and lost a night's pay to give you something I could get fired over." He looked at her thoughtfully. "I can't explain why I'm attracted to you and not to her—but there it is."

He sounded genuine, and Shannon found she believed him. But she couldn't imagine the two of them having anything in common.

"As I said, Steve, I'm very grateful for everything you did for me."

"And?"

"And I'm flattered."

"But you think it's a case of an inexperienced younger man lusting after an older woman."

She shook her head—but that was exactly what she thought.

Reading her mind, he said, "If you won't give me a chance to erase that erroneous picture, you'll be depriving yourself of something you'll wish you hadn't missed out on.''

''I'll think about it.'' That was all she'd do. No one could compare to David. No one.

''You do that. I'll wait to hear from you. Ciao.''

With her first goal accomplished, she left the restaurant and drove to Blue Spruce Drive. Amy had warned her she shouldn't do anything until Jack Casey called her back. But that might take a long time. Shannon couldn't see how it would hurt to see where he lived.

If her twin was his wife or his sister, then Shannon wanted to find out how she'd lived all these years. If her twin was his girlfriend, she wanted to see what kind of man her sister was dating.

After asking directions several times, she finally found the address. It was on the outskirts of Portland in a lovely wooded area. Blue Spruce Drive itself was a long, sweeping road lined with evergreens. Every so often, she glimpsed an estate surrounded by acres of private property. Whoever the Caseys were, they had money.

When she found the mailbox, she took a left up the winding drive. It was still light out and she drove slowly, gazing around her. Taking one more bend, she could see a large, beautiful contemporary home in the distance. The people who lived here led a life of great comfort and luxury.

This was as far as she dared go. Noting a driveway leading to an enormous garage, she turned into it, intending to reverse the car and head back to the road. A sandy-haired young man of medium height suddenly came out one of the doors. For a brief instant their eyes met.

"CC!" he called. "Wait up! Where's your MG? Did you buy a new car?"

You've done it now, Shannon.

He walked to the driver's side and peered in. She saw recognition dawn. "You're my sister's twin! I thought you were going to wait until I called you back."

"I have been waiting, and I planned to continue waiting. But I was in town today for an interview at Sacred Heart Hospital, and I decided to satisfy my curiosity by driving out here. As you could see, I was turning around when you came out the door. I wasn't going to approach anyone."

"Be that as it may, you took a risk that could hurt a lot of people. Drive back to the Sacred Heart Emergency parking lot. I'll meet you there."

"All right."

She took off as fast as she could. Jack Casey was her twin's brother! The last thing she wanted to do was upset him.

Long before she reached the hospital, he'd passed her in his Porsche. The man drove too fast, but she had to admit he handled speed like a pro. When she saw him parked at the far end of the lot, she pulled in next to him.

He got out of his car and walked toward the passenger side of her Jetta. She unlocked the door for him.

He slipped inside and began speaking without preamble. "As you know, my name is Jack Casey. And you're Shannon White."

She nodded.

Once more his eyes made a meticulous sweep of her body, from her hair to her feet.

"Are we as identical as Steve said we were?"

"Yes."

Tears filled her eyes. "Thank God I've found her. Does she know she has a twin sister?" Shannon asked eagerly.

"Yes."

Shannon's spirits plummeted. The talk with David came flooding back.

Maybe she knows she's adopted. Maybe she knows she's a twin. But what if it doesn't mean anything to her? That's entirely possible.

"How long have *you* known you were a twin?" Jack Casey asked her.

"My parents adopted me when I was an infant. But it wasn't until my widowed mother was dying a year ago that she told me I had a twin. That's all she said.

"I didn't know if it was a boy or a girl. I wasn't even sure if the whole thing was a figment of her imagination. There were no documents or papers for me to check."

"Do you have other brothers or sisters, Shannon?"

"No. I was an only child. What about my twin?"

"She has two brothers besides me."

"You call her CC?"

He nodded. "Her name is Catherine."

"Catherine Casey. That's a beautiful name. She has three brothers? What a lucky girl!"

"Are you dating the waiter at the Crompton Steakhouse? Is that why he was willing to give you information?"

"Oh, no. But since he mentioned seeing you with my twin, I asked him to help me find her and he obliged. I can tell you're upset, but please don't blame him."

"I don't. So who was the man you were with when you went to dinner there the first time?"

She averted her eyes. "David Britton of the Britton Institute. I'm in love with him and had hopes our relationship would end in marriage. I would give anything in the world to be his wife. But apparently he's met someone else since we were together. He says it's serious."

She swallowed hard. "I'm rambling. Sorry. You've caught me at an emotional moment."

"I'm sorry I caught you at all." Jack half-grimaced, half-smiled. "Unfortunately what I have to tell you is going to be even more painful."

"You mean your sister doesn't want to meet me."

"That's right. It's nothing personal. It couldn't be."

His words killed the hope in her heart. "Are you going to tell her you've met me?"

"No. I'm not going to do anything. It'll have to

be up to her to decide if she ever wants to make contact with you.''

''Then it could be a long wait.''

''It might never happen.''

''I realize that now.''

He cocked his head. ''What do you mean *now?*''

''The man I'm in love with warned me how delicate and complicated the situation is when one twin isn't looking for her sibling.''

''Take my word for it. In this case, it *is* complicated. And delicate. If it's any consolation, I hope she decides to look you up one day.''

''I do, too.'' Her voice trembled. ''Thank you for being kind enough to meet me here and talk to me.''

''Now I feel guilty,'' Jack muttered.

''Why?''

''Because in coming here, I'm afraid I've caused you to spend the rest of your life waiting. Don't do it. Don't wait for something that might never happen. Goodbye, Shannon.''

''Wait—'' She reached into the back seat for the manila envelope Steve had returned to her. ''Please take this. It has a picture and some information about me. In case she ever feels curious…''

She thought he was going to ignore her. But at the last second, he took it from her hands and got out of the car. Before she'd had a chance to back out of her spot, his Porsche had shot away like an arrow in flight.

CHAPTER EIGHT

SATURDAY'S RACE was over. Catherine and the rest of her family, including Mark and Brody, waited for Jack and Melanie to arrive at the house. Their mother had planned a victory dinner for him.

When Catherine glanced out the living room window, she could see a couple of the crew parking Jack's race car in the garage. She waited until she saw his Porsche, then hurried out of the house and down the drive to congratulate him on his win.

Today's race had helped pass the time. For Catherine, this had been the longest, loneliest week of her life. No number of phone calls or flowers from David could take the place of being in his arms. But the wait was almost over, and she was euphoric. Later tonight, he'd be coming by her condo. Meanwhile, she would enjoy this celebration with her family.

As she entered through the side door of the garage, Jack and Melanie were getting out of his car.

"That was a terrific win today! I got it all on the camcorder."

They both turned. Melanie was beaming, but Jack's normal victory smile was missing.

"It was great to see the whole family at the track today. It meant a lot to me."

He said the right words, but he sounded strange. His eyes played over her face, as if he hadn't seen her for a long time and needed to take a good, hard look.

"David not back yet?" he asked.

"No. I don't expect him until later this evening."

"That's good, because there's something Melanie and I need to tell you before you see him again." She'd hoped they were going to announce their engagement, but with that comment, some of her happiness evaporated.

"What's wrong, Jack?"

She noticed he was out of breath, as if he'd been running a great distance. Now that she studied him more closely, she saw that he looked pale, and there were beads of perspiration near his hairline.

When he didn't answer, she began to feel real anxiety. "Can't it wait until dinner's over?"

"It could. But we don't want to take the chance that David might come by the house before you hear what we have to say."

Melanie looked at her with compassion.

"Hear *what?*"

"On Wednesday evening, Shannon drove by our property, just looking around. But I caught her. We had a short, private talk. It seems David had a relationship with her before he ever met you."

"No, he didn't. You must have misunderstood. He told me that when Shannon came to the institute in response to the ad, he took her out to dinner to interview her. After that night he never saw her again. End of story."

He shook his head. "She tells a slightly different tale."

"Then she's lying!"

She saw Melanie and Jack exchange private glances.

"Maybe she is, CC. I hope she is, because I know how much you love David. I think he's pretty special, too." He paused, shrugged, averted his eyes.

"Still…" he continued. "When you see him later, just ask him if he's told you the whole truth about his relationship with her."

"They didn't have one," Catherine insisted. "It exists only in her imagination."

"Catherine?" Melanie said quietly. "Apparently she's in love with David. She told Jack that until you came along, she was planning to marry him."

Tears stung Catherine's eyes. "I don't believe it."

"We don't want to believe it, either," Jack muttered. "You know how much I love you, CC. We only told you this as precaution because we don't want to see you get hurt. If it's a lie on her part, then you'd have nothing to lose by asking him. But it's your call."

"I don't need to ask him. I trust him completely."

He stared at her for a long moment. "If you trust him, then that's good enough for me. We'll never bring it up again. Let's go. I'm starving!"

Catherine held back.

"You two go on."

She saw alarm in his expression. "Where are you going?"

"I've decided I'm going to wait for David at my place. Tell everybody I'm sorry, but I'm too excited about seeing him to be good company."

She dashed past them and climbed into her MG. Her tires squealed on the pavement as she tore down the drive. The warm July evening was beautiful, but she was crying so hard it might as well have been raining. Catherine could barely see and had to pull over more than once.

Call me, David. I've never needed anyone in my life like I need you tonight.

As soon as she arrived at her condo, she checked her answering machine in case David had called after she'd left. Desolate when she didn't hear his voice, she threw herself on the bed and sobbed.

In a little while, the buzzer sounded. She sat up to listen. It buzzed a second, then a third time. She flew through the hall to the door.

"Who is it?"

"David!" It was his deep, familiar voice.

Her fingers were clumsy as she unfastened the bolt. Before she could completely open the door, he shouldered himself inside.

"Catherine!" he cried as he drew her into his arms.

Aching for this closeness after a deprivation that felt like months instead of days, she lifted her head. They kissed again and again with an unquenchable thirst. No kiss was long enough or deep enough. The miracle of two bodies coming together like this blotted out the world.

Her body was molded to his, driven by a force she couldn't control and didn't want to. "If I'd had to wait one more minute for you to come home—" Feverish with need, she covered his face with tiny kisses. Her lips had a life of their own as they traveled over eyelids and nose, sampling the masculine texture of his skin.

His mouth chased after hers, kissing the very breath out of her. "I'm never leaving you again."

"Please, let's get married right away."

The dark blue eyes she adored were charged with new light. "I've had September first circled on my calendar since we met. It's a Saturday."

She smiled before giving him another hungry kiss. "I was thinking much sooner than that."

His hands stilled on her face. "Any sooner, and we wouldn't be able to plan the kind of wedding I'm sure your parents have in mind for their only daughter."

"I don't want a big one. All I care about is being with you. Didn't you say something about driving to Nevada?"

"I did say that, and I'd take you there in a second if I thought you really meant it. But you know as well as I do that it would disappoint your family. Even though it's going to be hell, I can wait another month for the privilege of becoming your husband. I'd like everything legal before I start making love to my wife the way I want to—and the way I will for the rest of our lives.''

''Our honeymoon…'' she said breathlessly.

''I have access to a villa with a private beach on one of the Greek islands. The crowds will be gone by September. That's where I've dreamed of us spending our honeymoon.''

''It sounds wonderful!''

He reached in his trousers pocket and pulled out a ring. It was the exquisite pear-shaped diamond they'd chosen, mounted in white gold. Finding her left hand, he pushed it onto her ring finger, then kissed her palm.

His eyes narrowed on her features. ''I've been waiting all week to put this ring on your finger. You have no idea how much I love you. Come here to me, Catherine.''

She threw her arms around his neck, needing no urging. While the passion flared between them, she couldn't hear Jack and Melanie's voices.

David had a relationship with her before he ever met you.

Ask him if he's told you the whole truth.

She's in love with David.

Until you came along, she was planning to marry him.

WHEN CATHERINE met him at the door, her response had been everything he could have hoped for. But her suggestion that they get married in Nevada as soon as possible wasn't in character.

His gut always told him when something was wrong. Though she'd accepted his ring, he knew there was definitely something wrong. The only thing to do was get it out of the way before it grew larger. Expose it—confront it. She'd agreed to marry him. He didn't want any shadows darkening his universe.

They moved to the couch, where he pulled her onto his lap, pleased to see that the red roses he'd sent her had been placed on the coffee table. Their heavy scent filled the room.

She buried her face against his neck. "How was the trip? How did things go with your mom?"

"It did her a world of good. We were finally able to talk about the past. She cried when Mitch and I told her what we'd discussed with the doctor. Before we got home, she agreed to make an appointment with him."

Catherine hugged him tighter. "That's wonderful."

"She's expecting you for dinner tomorrow. Seeing that diamond on your finger will give her another reason to get up to a new day."

In answer, Catherine kissed him with the kind of passion he had no defense against.

"Darling? If tonight's the night you want to make love for the first time, there's nothing I'd like more. But before I carry you in the bedroom, I need to know what's bothering you."

He felt her draw in a deep breath as she straightened.

"Look at me," he whispered.

Slowly she turned her head until they could stare into each other's eyes. Hers looked haunted. He didn't have to ask.

This had to do with her twin.

"Are you still feeling guilty because you don't want to meet your twin?"

She averted her eyes.

"It's all right, Catherine. Let's talk about what's really upsetting you."

He could see her throat working. "Shannon came out to the house this week. Jack saw her in her car and they talked. Apparently your name came up in the conversation."

David had known Shannon couldn't let it go. An icy chill crept through his body. "Go on."

"According to Shannon, you and she had a relationship before you ever met me. I told Jack what you told me. That you'd taken her to dinner once, and then you'd never seen her again.

"Jack said Shannon intimated it was more than that. She says she's in love with you. She told him she was planning to marry you until I entered the picture. I told him it had to be a lie. That was good enough for Jack. He told me he'd never bring it up again."

Lord help me.

"Look at me, Catherine."

Once again she shifted her eyes to his.

"As God is my witness, Shannon and I never had a relationship."

She grasped his hand in both of hers. "I knew it!"

"But— I haven't told you everything about that night."

The shattered look on Catherine's face tore him to pieces.

"Dear God." Tears spurted from her eyes. "Please don't tell me you slept with her. Please don't." She started to pull away from him, but he held on to her.

"I won't, because it never happened. It never *could* have happened. That was the problem. I wasn't attracted to her that way."

Catherine brushed away the tears with her fingers. "And she was? Attracted to you, I mean?"

"Yes."

"You didn't sense this before you asked her out to dinner?"

What he said now would upset her. But he knew he'd never be able to live with himself if he didn't tell her the whole truth. This woman deserved his total honesty.

"When people come to the institute to be a participant in our study, I often do the initial interview."

"I know. You've already told me."

"This was different. In order to understand, you have to step outside yourself, to a time before you and I met. Will you try?"

After a long silence, she said, "Yes."

"When Louise told me we had a drop-in, I asked

her to send the person to my office. It turned out to be Shannon White from Tacoma, Washington. There was only one word to describe her. As Mitch would say, she was a gorgeous, knockout blonde.''

At this point Catherine slid off his lap. He had no choice but to let her go. Her body rigid, she faced him from a few feet away.

''I felt an immediate attraction to her. It was physical, of course. That's all it could be. I didn't know her! Since I started the institute, I'd never dated anyone who worked for me or came in as a volunteer.

''But in her case I made an exception and I asked her out to dinner. She seemed so eager to accept, I realized the chemistry was working for her, too. It was my way of mixing business and pleasure—enjoying an evening with a lovely woman *and* getting the information we needed.''

Her moist gray eyes stared at him as if he were a completely unknown quantity to her.

''I picked her up at her hotel and we drove downtown. She'd only come to Portland a few times before. I'd been so impressed by the renovation of the Crompton warehouse, I decided to take her to dinner there. Someone at work recommended the steakhouse.

''As the evening progressed, I began my official interview with her. Naturally I learned a lot about her in a comparatively short period of time. But the date fell far short of my expectations.''

David could tell that every word of explanation distanced Catherine a little more.

"Let me ask you a question. In the past, have you ever been out with a man you really wanted to get to know, but at some point you realized you weren't interested, after all?"

He waited to go on until she'd nodded.

"That experience is exactly what happened to me. As good-looking as she was, as intelligent, that vital emotional connection was missing. It was so odd because the initial attraction had been stronger than anything I'd felt in years.

"You have to understand something else. For the first few minutes in my office, I'd thought maybe she was the one."

Catherine seemed to retreat even further, but he had to go on. He had to finish.

"When dinner was over, I took her back to her hotel. While we stood talking outside the door, she invited me in. I've never slept with a woman on a first or second date. But I might have gone into that room with her if I'd felt the desire.

"I kept wondering why I didn't. I thought maybe something was wrong with me. How could I blow so hot at the office, and then so cold at dinner? Since I was the instigator of our date, it didn't seem fair to her. Maybe I was too tired or too focused on my work. I worried that I wasn't giving her—us—enough of a chance. I thought if I kissed her, maybe I would find the elusive compon—"

"Passionately?"

"Yes."

Catherine tried to stifle a moan, but he heard it

and got to his feet, anxious to reassure her. She backed away. Where Catherine was concerned, that was a new experience for him, and it hurt.

"The one and only kiss I gave her meant less than nothing to me. In fact, it turned me off so completely, I had my answer. She wasn't the right woman for me at all. I'd made a mistake.

"Naturally, at that point I was sorry I'd asked her out, because I don't like hurting anyone. I also regretted having broken my rule about socializing with anyone connected with work.

"I told her that if we were ever contacted by someone whose picture and data matched hers— someone who was searching for a twin—the institute would get in touch with her right away. I told her goodbye, Catherine, not good-night. She couldn't have been under any illusion that I wanted to see her again.

"Unfortunately I didn't anticipate that she'd fantasize about something that never got off the ground. The next day she phoned my office wanting to take me to lunch. I put her off. She phoned other times, even came to Portland on a Friday afternoon hoping to take me to dinner. Again I had to tell her I was busy.

"When the waiter told her she had a double, she came to my office to discuss with me how she planned to find you." In a few words, he told Catherine what advice he'd given Shannon. "She left, and I haven't seen or talked to her since.

"Now you know the whole truth. All of it."

Her silence defeated him.

"Do you believe me, Catherine?"

"Yes," she answered in a wooden voice. "I still shiver when I recall the look in your eyes at the speedway. It was almost...revulsion. You thought I was Shannon. I remember driving away thinking how awful it would be if a man I cared about ever looked at me that way."

Relieved the truth was out in the open at last, he reached for her. But she raised her hands to ward him off.

"Don't touch me right now, David. I need time alone. Please leave. You'd better take this with you." She pulled off her diamond and returned it to him with an unsteady hand.

Incredulous, he held the ring between his fingers. It was still warm. "I thought the truth would clarify everything," he said as unemotionally as he could. "What's going on in your mind?"

Her eyes filled with tears. "How can you ask me a question like that? Earlier tonight I was ecstatic. I was so happy...."

"I felt the same way when I slid this ring on your finger. I still do."

She shook her head. "Everything's changed."

"Of course it hasn't! You admit you're in love with me, and I've just asked you to be my wife!"

"That was before."

"Before what?" he demanded. "Are you telling me you've never kissed another man and then regretted it?"

"No!" she cried, "but he didn't happen to be your identical twin brother!"

"Catherine, when I met Shannon I didn't even know you existed. She and I shared one dinner. Whatever I felt for her was over by the time I'd kissed her. I'm sorry if that sounds brutal, but it's the truth.

"When I met you, something wonderful happened to me. Something I can't explain. Yes, you looked like Shannon. I've already told you how strongly I was attracted to her appearance. But when you smiled at me and told me I'd mistaken you for someone else, I felt the essence of *you*. I sensed right away that you were nothing like Shannon.

"Don't get me wrong, Catherine. I'm sure she's a wonderful woman in her own right. If I sound callous about her, I don't mean to. But she isn't *you*.

"I wish to God she'd never come to the institute looking for her twin. But she did. It's a fact of life. It's also a fact of life that you and I met accidentally at the speedway.

"Don't you understand that it was *your* spirit I responded to, *your* charm? It drove me to look for you. Eventually I would have found you, with or without Mitch's help. As far as I'm concerned, it was destiny that we met again at the building site. I fell in love with you on the spot. And *you* fell in love with me. Don't you dare deny it!"

"I'm not denying anything."

"Then why all this anguish?"

She buried her face in her hands. "I wish I knew."

He struggled for breath. "Catherine, when I was in college, my best friend and I met two sisters at a football game. They were both cute, about eleven months apart. He was attracted to the older one, and I liked the younger one, so everything seemed fine.

"We went for pizza afterward. By the end of the night, my friend was starting to make moves on my date. At first I was angry because I liked the girl I was with a lot. But as time wore on, I could see she had feelings for my friend, too.

"They didn't plan for it to happen. It just did. Today they're happily married with three children. The older sister met someone later, and she's married, as well. The point is, no one can *create* the connection between two people. It's there or it's not."

She wiped her eyes with the backs of her hands. "You can't compare that situation to ours!"

The pain in her eyes seemed to accuse him. "You were so attracted to my twin, you took her out and kissed her the same night. Within a week you were attracted to me. It just took you a little longer to get around to kissing me."

Good Lord. "That's because I knew I'd found the woman for me. I didn't want to make any mistakes."

"David!" she cried in exasperation. "I'm not talking about the time it took to kiss me. I'm talking about *all* of it. Everything! Don't you see? I'm not sure you even *know* who you love or don't love. It's too weird, too bizarre.

"This is wrong! *We're* wrong!" Tears dripped off her pale cheeks. "Please, if you have any feeling for me, just leave. Please—" she begged.

Five minutes must have passed while he stood there, reeling from the possibility that he might truly have lost her.

"I'll go." In a few swift strides he was out the door.

CATHERINE WAITED until she was sure he'd driven away. Then she grabbed her purse and left the condo for her parents' home.

She picked up her cell phone from the passenger seat and punched in Jack's number. *Be there, Jack. Please be there.*

There was no answer.

She floored the accelerator, uncaring if the police caught her on radar. By some miracle she reached her parents' place without being pulled over. After parking her MG, she peered inside Jack's garage. Relieved to discover his Porsche was there, she raced toward the house.

"Catherine, darling!" her mother called out from the stairs. She was apparently on her way to bed. "What are you doing here so late? I thought you'd be with David."

"I said goodbye to him a little while ago."

Her mom frowned. "Goodbye?" She hurried over to Catherine and hugged her. "Obviously, something's wrong. You've been crying. What is it? Do you want me to get your father? I'm sure he's not in bed yet.''

''There *is* something wrong, Mom. It's so awful, I—I feel like I'm in a nightmare. But before I explain to you and Dad, I have to talk to Jack.''

''As far as I know, he and Melanie are still in the lounge watching the videos you took of today's race.''

''Good. Is it all right if I stay here tonight?''

''Since when do you have to ask a question like that?''

''Thanks, Mom. I'm sorry I wasn't here for the party. I promise I'll tell you everything in a little while.''

''I'm going to hold you to that.'' She kissed her daughter's forehead before starting up the stairs once more.

Jack met Catherine as she walked to the lounge. ''I thought I heard your voice.'' His sympathetic gaze took in her tears.

''Oh, Jack—'' While she stood there sobbing, he gave her a comforting hug, then led her to a chair.

When she could finally control herself, she said, ''It seems Shannon had her reasons for saying what she did, after all.''

''Did he have an affair with her?''

''No. But after he told me everything, I asked him to leave.''

''You two broke up?''

''Yes.''

"But if he didn't have an affair, and you believe him, then I don't get it."

"You don't understand." She let out a tormented groan. "I think this might be something only a woman understands. I need to talk to Mom."

They both looked as ill as she felt. "I'll go get her," Jack said, sprinting out of the room.

Melanie walked to her and hugged her without saying anything. A few minutes later, her parents entered the lounge and sat on the other couch.

Her mother said, "Jack told us you've broken up with David. That was all he would tell us. What happened, honey?"

Catherine sank back in her chair. There was no easy way to start this. Maybe the best thing to do was just forge ahead.

"When you adopted me, did you know I had an identical twin sister?"

If it hadn't been such a serious question, the blank expression on their faces might have been comical.

"Just as I thought. You had no idea."

Her dad straightened. "What's this all about?"

She rubbed her forehead, where she could feel a headache coming on.

"It started at the speedway three weeks ago, when I accidentally bumped into David in the bleachers. He mistook me for a woman he called Shannon."

Suddenly everything, the whole story, came out in a rush of emotion. Though she saw them exchange glances several times throughout the long, detailed explanation, her parents didn't interrupt.

"I know David's upset, but he has no comprehension of what this news has done to me. He begged me to help him understand my feelings. That's the problem. I can't put them into words yet. All I know is, our being together doesn't seem right. For want of a better word, I—I feel...unclean."

She felt a sense of relief that everything was out in the open. No more secrets. Her parents knew; they could help her figure out why she felt this way. But the longer the silence lasted, the more frightened she grew. She'd never known her parents to be at a loss for words.

She kept waiting for her father to chuckle and tell her she was making a mountain out of a molehill. Normally, her mother had a ready answer that lifted her spirits. Jack and Melanie sat on the other couch, clutching hands without saying anything.

"Well," she said shakily, "don't everyone speak at once."

Her father darted Jack a searching glance. "There's absolutely no question in your mind that this Shannon is Catherine's identical twin?"

Jack shot to his feet. "I'll let you be the judge of that. Be right back."

Catherine was in so much turmoil she hardly noticed his departure.

Never in her life could she recall the three of them sitting together without saying one word. She supposed she'd never seen her parents in shock before.

She remembered the pain in David's eyes when

she'd given him back the ring. The pain when she'd begged him to go.

"Here. Take a look for yourselves."

Jack returned and placed a paper in their father's outstretched hand. Cameron studied the picture thoroughly before handing it to their mother. She took one look and gasped. They both stared at Catherine.

She wiped her eyes. "May I see it?"

Her mother started to pass it to Catherine, but Jack forestalled her and held on to it. "This isn't a good idea, CC. You've already decided you're not going to meet her, so there's no point."

"I still want to see her."

"Mom? Dad? I already warned Shannon she shouldn't wait for CC to contact her. She's resigned to that fact. Why don't you just let it go, CC?"

"I didn't say I wanted to visit her. I just need to look at it. Where did you get it, anyway?"

"She gave it to me when she came to the house. But if you look at it, you'll torment yourself all over again with the knowledge that David knew her before he knew you. No way am I going to let you drive the dagger into your heart any deeper than it already is!"

"Your brother's right, Catherine." Her father intervened. "If you don't want to meet her, then don't look at it. You're about to open Pandora's box. You might not be ready for what you find."

She shook her head. "I have to see her."

"Here you go." Jack smiled at her sadly. "Just

be aware that we're all worried about you. You take this step, and everything's going to change.''

''It already has.'' Her voice shook as she held out her hand for the picture.

In Mitch's words, she's a gorgeous, knockout blonde.

CHAPTER NINE

WITH TREMBLING FINGERS Catherine raised it, then stared at her family. "Is this some kind of joke? Where's her picture?"

Lines darkened her father's face. "You're looking at it."

She let out an angry laugh. "This is the same picture on *my* driver's license. That's my blouse. Please don't tease me. Not about this."

"Open your wallet, honey," her mother suggested gently. "Then compare them."

Quickly she reached into her purse and extricated her license from its protective cover. She held both up. "They're exactly—"

But Catherine didn't finish what she was going to say. The smile in her picture was fuller than the smile in the other one.

"This is Shannon?"

Jack nodded soberly.

"She *is* me." Catherine couldn't take it in. "I feel sick."

Her mother flew over to her. "Quick, honey. Sit on the edge of the chair and put your head between your legs. You're in shock. It'll pass. Just keep your head down. Jack, get your sister some water."

"I couldn't drink it," she said shakily. "I'd throw it up."

After a few minutes, the light-headedness started to pass. Slowly she lifted her head.

Compelled to look at the pictures again, she started to laugh. "If Shannon and I stood side by side, David wouldn't know which one of us he wanted." She knew she was becoming hysterical, but she couldn't seem to stop.

Her father had come over to put his arms around her. He rocked her until the laughter turned to tears.

"CC," Jack murmured. "It's not the end of the world. He didn't have an affair with her."

"No. I don't have to worry about that. He came absolutely clean with me about everything. In fact, he was so honest, it almost killed me."

"Tell us what he said," her dad urged, sitting on the arm of the chair.

Catherine repeated everything she could remember. "The thing is, even if the connection he *wanted* to feel wasn't there, he still kissed her with passion to try and resurrect his initial feelings. He wanted the relationship that much!

"So where does that leave me? When he's kissing me, is it Shannon he really wants, because he was attracted to her first? But it's my kisses that turn him on? It makes me sick!"

"Did you tell him that?"

"Not in those exact words. I gave him back the ring."

Jack's eyes widened. "What ring?"

"That's right." Sniffling, she raised her head. "I forgot to tell you and Melanie. David and I became officially engaged tonight. We were planning our wedding for September first."

More hysterical laughter escaped. "I'd say our engagement was probably the shortest one on record. I think it lasted about an hour, maybe an hour and ten minutes."

Jack shook his head. "What a hell of a mess. The poor guy was damned no matter what he did."

"What do you mean?"

"He's madly in love with you, CC. Tonight he poured out his guts to you. He didn't *have* to tell you the truth. A man with that kind of honesty goes way up in my estimation."

Her father heaved a sigh. "I agree."

Tears trickled down her cheeks. "All along, I was too in love to be objective. I wish I'd never met him. I wish I didn't know I had a twin."

"We can blame our good friend Steve, the waiter. His interference ultimately placed David in this position."

"It doesn't matter who's to blame," she cried out. "He took her to dinner first, kissed her first. I can't get those images out of my mind. They ruin what I thought David and I had together."

She reached for her license and put it away. After hesitating, she picked up the photograph again. "What's she like, Jack?"

"We didn't talk for more than a few minutes.

Obviously she goes where angels fear to tread, but she's nice.''

Her mother took it from her. ''It's hard to believe this isn't your picture, honey. She even has the same kind of blouse you have! The one with the embroidery on the collar. It matches your blue sweater.''

''I know. That was the outfit I wore to the speedway the day I met David. She might even have been wearing the same thing when he first met her. Can you begin to understand how strange this all is?''

''Your adoption papers never mentioned that you were one of two live births,'' their father muttered, deep in thought. ''Believe me, we would have taken Shannon, too, if we'd known.''

Her brother let out a sigh. ''It was my lucky day that you didn't.''

''It was our lucky day, honey,'' Robyn assured him.

Cameron rubbed his head. ''For my own satisfaction, if nothing else, I'm going to contact the attorney who handled your adoption and see if he can find out more information for us.''

''How sad you two girls were separated.'' Catherine's mother eyed her tenderly. ''When you were very young and got mad at Jack over something, you used to tell me you wished you had a sister.''

''I didn't really mean it.''

''To think all along your identical twin was alive and well in Tacoma, Washington. Twenty-eight years you've been deprived of the knowledge of each other's existence. Incredible.''

Cameron got to his feet. "It's a damn shame David Britton is caught in the middle of this. Now that I know the background, I can understand he had compelling reasons for keeping quiet until now."

"Dad? It would have devastated me no matter when he chose to tell me."

"How can we help you, honey? What do you want to do?"

"I don't honestly know, Mom."

"Is Shannon aware that you're the woman David loves?"

"No. David told me that when she came to his office with the news that her twin had been seen at the restaurant, she asked him to go to dinner with her to talk about it some more.

"That's when David declined. He told Shannon he was in love with another woman and planned to get married. But he didn't name me, because he wanted to save her unnecessary pain.

"You see, I'd already told David I had no interest in meeting my twin. He assumed Shannon and I would never get together, so there was no point in telling her."

Impatiently Catherine dashed the tears from her eyes. "It's a nightmare. I don't know what to do."

"There's no black or white to a situation like this," Robyn said, sounding far away. "This is only an observation, honey, but as long as you don't have any desire to meet your twin, I can't see you resolving your feelings for David."

Cameron slanted her a penetrating glance. "It's

all a matter of how deeply you love this man. How much are you willing to risk?''

Catherine felt as if she'd been thrown off a ship to flounder in these stormy seas. ''I've got to be alone for a while,'' she said abruptly. She rose to her feet and slung her purse over her shoulder.

Everyone got up and walked her to the door. Her parents stood arm in arm. ''Whatever decisions you make, this family will always support you. We love you, honey.''

She nodded. ''I know you do. I'm the luckiest person in the world to have you for my parents.''

''Ditto for me,'' Jack muttered.

Melanie kissed her goodbye. ''Call me if you need to talk,'' she whispered.

DAVID CHECKED his car clock. Quarter after two. Catherine hadn't returned to her condo. He'd driven past her parking spot a dozen times in the past two hours.

She wasn't answering her cell phone. He had no doubt she was with her parents. Considering the state she was in, they'd probably insisted she sleep over. If that was the case, there was no point in waiting for her.

But until he could talk to her again, there was no point to his life, so he might as well stay put. If she hadn't come home by morning, he'd go to his condo and get ready for church. Maybe he'd find her there. He was prepared to do whatever it took.

He felt so wired, every time a resident of the

building pulled in for the night, his heart jumped a mile. To keep from thinking, he'd switched on the radio, choosing an all-news station. It hadn't done any good, but the noise was company of a sort.

As the two-thirty station break was announced, he saw her MG turn into the drive leading to her parking space. He shut off the radio and quietly left the car.

She got out of hers and started walking toward the lobby. In the moonlight her hair shone like gossamer.

"Catherine?" He called to her from several yards away.

He heard her gasp before she spun. A gentle breeze had sprung up, molding her dress to the curves of her body, outlining her slender legs.

"I didn't mean to startle you, but obviously it couldn't be helped. Please don't go in for a minute."

She hesitated. "How long have you been out here watching for me?"

"On and off for several hours, I feel like a criminal awaiting execution, but I don't know my crime. I've hurt you when I only meant to honor you by telling you the truth. Help me understand you, Catherine. I've known pain before, but never anything as excruciating as this.

"I love you. I can't bear the thought of losing you. I realize you need some time. But how much? When are you going to let me see you again?"

"I don't know." She sounded as though she was shivering. But the night was warm.

"What don't you know?"

"I saw her picture tonight."

"You're two completely different people."

"I thought it was *my* picture." She wasn't listening to him. "Do we kiss alike?"

"Don't do this, Catherine. You're torturing yourself over something that exists only in your imagination."

"I'm not surprised she's in love with you. If you kissed her the way you kissed me the first time, she'll never get over it."

A shudder ran through his body. "Whatever she thinks she feels, it isn't love. It couldn't be. She *will* get over it. But you and I aren't going to get over what we feel for each other."

"Be that as it may, she's my sister! My *twin!*"

"I know."

"What if I decide to meet her?"

"What if you do?" He fired the question back.

"She met you first. She loved you first."

"We'll deal with it."

"*How* do you deal with that?" she cried. "We're both in love with the same man! What do I tell her? Should I say, *I'm so sorry, Shannon. I know David liked you in the beginning. He's crazy about our looks, but for some reason he likes me better now. I hope you realize it's nothing personal.*"

David was dumbfounded. He might be aching for her, but there was no getting through to her tonight. It would take a much wiser person than he to understand her pain and confusion.

"Can I call you in a few days?"

"I'll call you when the blueprints are ready. I can't promise more than that."

"Catherine—"

"I—I have to go in."

AT EIGHT, David let himself inside his mother's house. He knew she would be up to start preparing their Sunday lunch.

"Mother? Are you upstairs or down?"

"David? I'm in the kitchen! What on earth are you doing over here this early?"

He found her at the sink and slid his arms around her. "Because there are times in a man's life when he needs his mother."

She turned to look at her son. "Darling, what is it?" She lifted a gentle hand to brush the hair from his brow.

"Catherine won't be coming to dinner. Could we sit down and talk? I need your perspective on this. Not only because you're a wise woman, but because you were a twin. There's no one I trust more than you to help me clarify things."

She moved to the table in the bay window overlooking her flower garden. He followed, and they sat. She patted his hand. "I don't recall your asking my help for anything since you were a boy."

"I feel like the time when I was in second grade, and this girl—Libby Marshall—came up behind me in the hall and knocked me down hard. I figured she must have hated me. To add insult to injury, she ran away laughing. I didn't dare tell anyone what had happened. But when I came home and talked to you about it, you said she did it because she liked me."

His mother nodded. "I remember that moment as if it were yesterday."

"Funny. I hadn't thought of it in years—not until just now. I think that was my first experience in trying to understand the female mind. Your explanation saved me a lot of mental grief growing up."

Her eyes filled with compassion. "What's gone wrong between you and Catherine?"

"First, I need to give you some background. Then maybe you can advise me on how to proceed, because frankly, I'm terrified we won't be getting back together."

He told her everything. His mother didn't stir until he'd finished describing his conversation with Catherine outside her condo.

"Twin sisters are complicated creatures," she said. "There can be a lot of wonderful sharing—a closeness unlike any other. There can also be more competition and jealousy between twins than between other sisters or friends.

"As you know, your aunt Colleen could never have children. Whenever we got together in the past, she never failed to remind me that I was the lucky one in the family, so stop complaining about losing Michael."

"Mother! I had no idea."

"It isn't something you talk about. Once I asked her why she didn't adopt. She bit my head off. When she and your uncle Ed moved to Detroit, I think she was secretly glad. That way she didn't have to be around me and you boys.

"I've missed her a lot, especially since your father died. The funny thing is, I know she misses me, too. We still talk on the phone every month or so because we have things to share that wouldn't mean anything to anyone else.

"But her envy of my life, of my ability to get pregnant, got in the way of any real closeness in our adult lives. The fact remains that she's never forgiven me for something that wasn't my fault. I daresay that if your aunt had been in love with your father, for instance, she would never have spoken to me again—because I married him.

"I know that's hard for you to understand, darling, because you're a man, and in my experience men usually get right down to the cold, hard facts.

"No doubt, it all seemed obvious to you. It's Catherine you love."

When he nodded, she went on. "You never made a commitment to Shannon. You never told her you loved her. The kiss didn't mean anything. Shannon knows that. Catherine knows that. None of this was your fault. So what could be more simple? Right?

"Wrong! You were talking to a woman last night. The more you tried to reason with her the way you might reason with another man, the more you lost ground. You were forgetting about the emotion involved here."

He rubbed the back of his neck. "I hear what you're saying. So where do I go from here?"

"She said she needs time. You're going to have to give it to her. She isn't always going to be confused like this. And I can promise you she's not going to fall out of love with you.

"But she's got some huge issues facing her. She knows she has a twin and she's terrified by that. Either she must ignore this knowledge completely, which at this point would be impossible, or she's going to have to take that leap of faith and meet her.

"If I don't miss my guess, she's already dying of curiosity to know the woman you were attracted to first."

"But what's she *really* afraid of?"

"Well, let me tell you something my doctor told me after the twins were born. You wouldn't remember but Colleen didn't come to the hospital, and she didn't want to see the babies after we brought them home."

"You're right. I don't recall her being around."

"I was very depressed because of it. He sat me down for a long talk about the fears of twin siblings.

"After what you've told me, if sounds like the neurotic part of Catherine is afraid. She's saying to herself, 'My twin is my other self, my other half. If David doesn't like Shannon, then why would he like me?'"

David sat forward. "So what you're saying is, she may hear me telling her I love her, but her fear is winning out."

"Like Colleen, Catherine is reacting defensively. Depending on a variety of factors, it may take her a long time to come around, especially if she's ever had a problem with trust."

"She has. There was a guy she met in college, a graduate student who pretended to be in love with her and stole some of her designs. Today she's a brilliant architect."

His mother nodded. "That college experience probably left her with doubts about herself—about her attractiveness...and her judgment. Maybe she'll see those inadequacies in her twin. Why would she want to come face-to-face with them? It would mean acknowledging them in herself.

"But there's safety in her profession, in her family, so why get married? Colleen found safety by staying away from anything that reminded her of the pain she felt in not being able to have children.

"Carrying this further, I can see why Catherine has never wanted to know about her birth parents or her twin. The rational side of her knows she's lucky to have been adopted by a wonderful family. But what if Shannon wasn't so lucky? What if she was forced to lead a reprehensible life? Catherine doesn't want to deal with the guilt she would feel."

"In what way?"

"If she discovers that her life was better than Shannon's, then she'll feel guilty that, for some reason, she was given everything and Shannon was given less. It's one of those 'There but for the grace of God go I' kind of things."

"You mean it's like the guilt Mitch felt for living when Michael died."

"Yes. She hasn't even met her twin yet, and already she's suffering tremendous guilt that her twin lost out in love. It's even more severe because the man who couldn't return her twin's love is in love with *her*.

"Catherine's soul is at war. In order to do penance, her honorable side says she must give you up for a nobler cause.

"Her emotional side doesn't want to believe that because she's in love with you. But she's afraid that if she gives in to her emotions, you'll find the other parts of her you didn't like in Shannon.

"I don't know anything about Shannon, but I do know about Colleen. Apparently her fears were much greater than mine. Maybe Shannon's are greater than Catherine's, which might explain your attraction to her instead of Shannon.

"I'm just guessing, but Shannon may have been let down in her romantic entanglements. Without any family left, she's reaching out to her twin for that human connection. This will play havoc with Catherine's guilt, as well. She has parents and brothers, *and* the prince."

"The prince?"

"Yes, darling. That's you. In Colleen's case, I was given children. The jewels in the crown of life. Colleen couldn't handle it."

David felt ill. He got up from the chair, raking a

hand through his hair. "You can't predict a good outcome for me, can you?"

"If I look back to the experience with Colleen, I would have to say no. But your situation is entirely different. Never underestimate the power of your love. As long as you have some understanding of Catherine's fears, it should help you cope as events unfold."

Cope.

After planning his wedding, he was now reduced to coping?

"Thanks for the talk, Mother."

"Oh—" Her eyes looked pained. "I'm afraid I've made things worse."

He shook his head. "No. You've explained a lot that didn't make sense before. Now I've got to go. Rest assured that you've been more help than you know. I'll talk to you soon."

After stopping at his condo to shower and shave, David headed for church. He might have allowed Catherine to get her own way last night, but today he had no intention of giving up on their relationship. Certainly he had every right to attend the same services she did.

Once he'd turned into the crowded church parking lot, he looked for her MG, but it was nowhere to be found. Refusing to let that discourage him, he parked and got out of the car.

Halfway through the service, he saw her slip into the back, and his breath caught. The sheen of her silvery-blond hair seemed to have a glow all its own.

She glanced around for a pew that wasn't crowded. When their eyes locked, she seemed to pale before she ran out.

He hurried after her, ignoring the curious gazes of the people around him. He was too late. She took off down the street in her MG, leaving him staring after her—just like that first time at the speedway.

There was no point in trying to catch up. His mother had said Catherine needed time. After her haste to get away from him, he finally accepted it.

But by Wednesday of the following week, he was crazy with pain and couldn't imagine living in this limbo much longer. Every time the phone rang, his heart slammed against his ribs in the hope that Catherine's agony over their separation had driven her to call him.

So far she hadn't tried to contact him. *Four days without seeing her, without holding her.* The idea of spending the coming weekend without her was too bleak to contemplate.

When he heard a tap on the door, his nerves were so on edge he jumped. Louise entered his office and closed the door behind her.

He couldn't prevent a curse.

Shannon had to be in reception, otherwise Louise wouldn't have that strange look on her face again.

"What's her excuse for wanting to see me this time?" He knew he sounded abrupt, but he was feeling desperate.

"She's come up with something new, Mr. Britton. I don't understand how she thinks I wouldn't remember her, but just now she introduced herself as Catherine Casey.'' David almost fell out of his chair. ''There really is something wrong with her, you know?''

He rose to his feet, trying to quell the frantic pounding of his heart. ''Does she have a portfolio with her?''

Louise blinked. ''No.''

The news made him euphoric.

''Tell her to come in.''

He was standing in the middle of his office when she walked in, wearing a tailored navy suit and white blouse he'd never seen before.

''Catherine—'' He couldn't say anything else, not another word. She was so damn beautiful it took his breath.

She wouldn't meet his gaze. ''Forgive me for barging in on you like this. I was afraid if—''

''If you had to talk to me first, you'd lose your nerve,'' he finished for her.

''Yes.''

''I want to take you in my arms, darling.''

''Please don't do that,'' she said. Her voice shook. ''I've come here to talk. If it's not convenient, I can—''

''What the hell do you mean, not convenient?'' He'd cut her off again. ''I *want* you to interrupt me. I've been praying for it!'' He moved past her to shut the door, then walked to his desk and told Louise to hold all his calls.

They stood facing each other like adversaries. She still refused to make eye contact with him.

"Please sit down!" she cried. "When you stand there like that, I can't—" She sucked in her breath. "I can't do this."

Summoning what little control he had left, he took his place behind the desk. Finally she lifted her eyes to his.

She was in as much pain as he was, but he couldn't rejoice in the fact.

"I've been doing a lot of soul searching," she began.

"So have I. My life means nothing without you," he said hoarsely. "I'll do anything it takes to get us back to where we were when I got home from my trip."

"I don't want that, David."

His eyes closed in renewed pain.

"When you first returned, I still didn't know the whole truth. Now that I do, nothing's the same anymore. I won't be able to think about our relationship until after I've met Shannon. It's something I'd hoped wouldn't come to pass, but circumstances have dictated otherwise. I've thought of a plan I think will work."

"And what is that?"

"Because you were the person Shannon first approached, you should be the one to phone her. You could say that because she volunteered your name to Jack, he contacted you to set up a meeting."

David's anger was kindled. "I'm not afraid to tell

Shannon the truth, Catherine. Especially not in front of you. In fact, I'm looking forward to it.''

"No!" she blurted. "That's exactly what I don't want you to do.''

"You mean you want her to go on believing I'm in love with someone other than you?''

"Yes! Promise me you won't tell her.''

"I can't do that. There's been enough unwitting subterfuge. If you want me to call her and arrange a meeting, I'll do that. But I'll tell her the truth about us first.

"It'll give her time to come to terms with the situation. Maybe then we can all begin to make sense out of this havoc and get on with our lives.''

She shook her head. "If your mind is made up about this, then I guess there's nothing more to be said.'' She jumped up from the chair.

David grasped her arm before she could reach the door. They were both out of breath.

"*Why* don't you want her to know about us?''

Her bottom lip trembled. He had the strongest desire to kiss it still, but knew he couldn't do that.

"Because it would hurt her.''

"Only superficially.''

"You're wrong. I've put myself in her place, and I know.''

"You think delaying the truth will hurt her any less?''

"Maybe she'll never have to learn the truth.''

He didn't like where this conversation was headed. "What are you saying?''

"I don't know exactly!" she cried. "Who can predict how any of this will turn out?"

"What's there to predict? We love each other."

Though his mother had talked to him about Catherine's fears, the fright and bewilderment in her eyes was beginning to panic him.

"We have to do this my way or not at all, David."

He knew she meant it.

Earlier he'd told her he would do whatever it took to get them back together.

He exhaled the breath he'd been holding. "All right. I'll call her and set things up."

"Since she has to drive from Tacoma, it should probably be on a Saturday."

"I'll see what I can arrange."

"When you know the date, call me."

"I'll come to your office and pick you up."

"No—"

A tortured moan accompanied her protest. As long as he could still wring that kind of emotion from her, it meant she was vulnerable. He would use that knowledge to his advantage. Heaven knew, he needed all the help he could get.

Without conscious thought he tilted her face with his hands. She knew what was coming and started to cry out, but he lowered his mouth over hers, stifling any sound.

Caught unawares, she stopped fighting and began to respond with all the ardor he could have hoped for. The taste and feel of her overwhelmed him. The fragrance of her hair and skin acted like an aphrodisiac to his senses.

"Come home with me now," he begged. "I love you. I want to be alone with you. Can't you see how much we need each other?"

She tore her lips from his, then staggered backward. Her eyes were glazed. "I knew this would happen if I saw you again! I've got to get out of here."

He felt he was losing his mind. "Why do you have to go? It doesn't make any sense!"

"What I'm doing is wrong," she whispered.

Before he'd had time to recover, she'd disappeared.

He moved to his desk and buzzed Louise.

"Yes, Mr. Britton?"

"I don't have any more appointments this afternoon, do I?"

"No, sir."

"Good. I'm leaving for the day. If you need me, just call me at home or on my cell phone."

"Of course." After a brief pause, she said, "I hope that woman won't bother you anymore."

"Louise, Catherine Casey can bother me whenever she wants. She's the woman I'm going to marry."

"That *wasn't* Shannon White?"

"No. Shannon White is Catherine's twin. It's a complicated story. One day I'll tell you about it." But not yet. Because right now this was a story in search of an ending....

CHAPTER TEN

TWENTY MINUTES LATER, David entered his condo and went directly to his study. He pulled out the little pocketbook he normally carried with him. Shannon had given him two numbers. He tried her home number first. When she wasn't there, he called her at work.

On the fourth ring, he heard, "Glen Cove Nursing Home. Ms. White speaking."

"Shannon? It's David Britton."

"David! It's so wonderful to hear your voice!"

Trying to ignore her effusive warmth, he said, "I'm glad I found you in your office. I have the news you've been waiting for. Your twin came to see me today. She wants to meet you."

"Oh, David! You don't know what this means!" He heard the joy in her voice before she broke down crying.

"Jack Casey put his sister in touch with me. She was thinking Saturday might be the best time to meet, because it might be more convenient for you."

"It wouldn't matter which day," she told him, her voice trembling. "I'd meet her anytime, anywhere."

"So if it was arranged for then, you could be at my office by, say, one o'clock?"

"I could be there today if you wanted. After what you've told me, I've decided to drive down from Tacoma on Friday and stay at that same hotel. Please, would you meet me there? This calls for a celebration. I want to buy you a drink in the bar."

His hand tightened around the receiver. "You know why I can't do that, Shannon."

"But this is my way of thanking you for helping me."

"I understand the person you really have to thank is Steve, the waiter at the Crompton steakhouse."

"I've already thanked him. I'm so excited I know I won't get any sleep for the rest of the week. Couldn't you and I at least meet for breakfast on Saturday? I want to repay you for everything you've done."

"That isn't necessary."

"Surely your fiancée would understand."

He recalled his words to Catherine and her reply.

You think delaying the truth will hurt her any less?

Maybe she'll never have to learn the truth.

"Shannon—just plan on being at my office at one."

The quiet on her end increased his guilt. He couldn't handle much more of this.

"All right," she said in a tear-filled voice. "I'll be there. Thank you."

There was a click.

The nightmare had entered a new phase.

He walked to the bar and poured himself a drink. After downing it in one gulp, he reached for his phone to call Catherine. As it turned out, she was still at her office.

"Hello, David. I saw it was you on the caller ID."

He swallowed hard. She'd schooled her voice to sound like her business self. After everything they'd shared, his first impulse was to tell her he was on his way over to see her, whether she liked it or not. But he couldn't do that, not after what he'd learned today.

"Catherine? I just got off the phone with Shannon. She'll be at my office on Saturday at one."

"This Saturday?" She sounded terrified. More than ever, he knew it was best to get this first meeting over with as soon as possible.

"Yes. That sounded fine to her."

There was no reply for a moment, but he could hear her shallow breathing. "I'm sure she was thrilled to hear from you," she finally said.

Don't, Catherine.

"Shannon's been waiting for this moment a long time. What I heard in her voice was excitement. She's finally going to meet her twin."

She took a shuddering breath.

"Catherine, she knows I'm in love with someone else and assumes I'm formally engaged. If she should bring up anything about my fiancée on Saturday, understand that I couldn't disabuse her of the fact that you gave me back the ring."

"She wanted to meet you alone, didn't she?"

He sucked in his breath. "Naturally she wanted to thank me for getting you two together."

"No. It goes much deeper than that."

Change the subject.

"Why don't we drive out of town somewhere tonight for dinner?"

"I can't. I—I've got to hang up."

He groaned inwardly. "I understand. If you feel like arriving early on Saturday, I'll be in my office by twelve-thirty. Call me on your cell phone and I'll come out to the front door to let you in. Good night, darling."

He hung up quickly, unable to bear hearing the click on her end first.

"CC? WE'RE GOING to be late if you don't get a move on."

"I can't decide what to wear."

Jack walked into her bedroom. "Good grief—this place is a mess! I can't even see the bed."

"Don't tease me right now, Jack. Do you like this café au lait jacket with my cream top and pants?" She'd bought it to wear to the race in Vancouver with David.

"You look great. Everything you wear looks great. Let's go."

"You don't understand."

"I know, I know—I'm a man. I get that from Melanie all the time. CC—the clothes aren't important. Okay? We have to go."

"Thank you for coming with me. I'm sorry it meant you had to miss today's race in Vancouver." They left the condo.

"I wouldn't let you do this alone. There's always another race. Anyway, what's a brother for?"

Catherine gave him a strained smile. "Where's Melanie? I thought she'd be with you."

"She had to work at the blood bank today because of some emergency."

They opened the doors of his Porsche and got in. "David must feel like he's in hell right about now."

At the mention of his name, her heart jumped. "I don't want to talk about him."

"The guy's suffering. Have a heart, CC."

"So am I."

Saturday traffic was always bad. Finding a place to park downtown was next to impossible. Jack used the building's underground car park, then escorted her to the elevators.

The building seemed fairly empty as she and Jack hurried down the hall and past Reception. But when they rounded the corner, Catherine froze.

Not five feet away, she saw her twin standing in front of David's office door. Catherine's first thought was that she was looking at herself in a mirror.

Shannon was dressed in the same cut of jacket as Catherine's, only it was part of a matching brown pantsuit with a cream top. They both wore bone-colored sandals and carried matching handbags.

Their hair had been cut in the exact same style, same length.

She hung back.

Her twin must have sensed people behind her because she turned to face them.

Catherine found herself staring into a pair of questing gray eyes as familiar as her own.

Dear God.

They continued to stare at each other without speaking.

"Are you all right?" Jack whispered.

"It's incredible, isn't it?" Shannon spoke first, then smiled.

"Yes. Utterly incredible."

David opened the office door. He wore a formal stone-gray suit, and Catherine held her breath, stunned again by how attracted she was to this man.

Instantly his gaze locked with hers. He sent her the private greeting she'd come to crave. It said he wished they were alone. It said he'd missed her. It said that now she was here, life had meaning again.

David—if you only knew.

"It looks like everyone's met. Come in."

The minute they stepped inside, Shannon grabbed David's arm and smiled at him with tears in her eyes. The love radiating from her ripped Catherine apart.

"When I came here last month, I hoped but never dreamed this day would come."

Catherine noticed how smoothly David eased

himself away by walking toward his inner office door and opening it.

"Well, now that the miracle has occurred, Jack and I are going to leave you to get acquainted while we go downstairs to the coffee shop. Take as long as you need. We'll bring you some coffee in a while."

"Don't panic," Jack whispered in Catherine's ear. "You two need time alone."

"Make yourselves at home, ladies."

The men left the suite.

Catherine thought she was going to be sick right then and there.

"I know you didn't want to meet me," Shannon began. "David told me to expect this reaction because you didn't know about me and haven't been looking for me.

"If you never want to see me after today, I'll understand. I'm not saying I'll like it—" her voice cracked and she took a deep breath "—but I'll live with it if I have to. It's just that my mother told me I had a twin somewhere. I didn't know if it was true or not. She was in the last stages of pneumonia. She said, 'Shannon—you have a twin. You have a twin.' Then she died.

"I've been trying to find you ever since. First Steve—the waiter—then your brother verified that what she'd told me was true. I was overjoyed to learn I had a sister. Not that I wouldn't have loved a brother, but I always wanted a sister.

"My adoptive parents were schoolteachers who

lived on a fixed income. They adopted me late in life and couldn't afford to adopt another child. Dad was a good man, but stern.

"After he died of a heart attack, my mother cried a lot. I know she regretted the fact that they didn't arrange to get another child, a sibling for me. But Dad felt that one was all they could handle, and she would never have gone against his wishes.

"I think it's the reason she hoped I'd find you some day. But I don't have any papers. I have no idea where we were born or how we got separated. Or why." Tears rolled down her cheeks. "But right now I'm so happy to be looking at you at last, nothing else matters.

"I was hoping we could be friends. If I want it, I've been offered a job as an administrative nurse at a hospital here in Portland. I applied for a position at the institute's clinic, but David told me it's against policy to employ a participant."

Her eyes beseeched Catherine. "There's nothing in this world I would love more than to live near family." She half-sobbed as she said, "This time it would be my very own flesh and blood."

Catherine could think of nothing to say. She felt numb, her emotions paralyzed.

"They say twins communicate before they're even born," Shannon went on. "I've been reading a lot about it. How their tastes are similar, their gestures. Look at our outfits, and our hair!"

Catherine had been looking. And listening.

She sank down in the nearest chair. "I admit this

has come as a shock," she began. "Your picture was exactly like my driver's license picture. We own the same outfit."

"The blouse with the embroidery on the collar? Blue?"

"Yes." She paused. "My parents had no idea I was a twin. Dad's working with the attorney who arranged for my adoption. They're going to try to find out what happened."

"That's marvelous! Maybe they'll learn the names of our birth parents. Oh, there's so much I want to know. So many questions to ask. What kind of work do you do?"

"I'm an architect."

"An architect—" The wonder in her voice humbled Catherine. "Did you design the home I saw when I met your brother?"

"Don't I wish! No. That's my father's creation. He's Cameron Casey, a renowned architect in the Northwest."

"I see. Does your mother work?"

"She gardens as a hobby—she's incredible. People come from miles around to see the grounds at our house. She can make anything grow." She gave Shannon a faint smile. "But I hear you're an administrative nurse with a master's degree. You run a whole nursing facility. That's an enormous responsibility."

"That's nothing compared to what you do. Maybe one of our relatives was Frank Lloyd Wright."

"Or Florence Nightingale," Catherine interjected in the same light tone, because it was either say that or have a nervous breakdown.

"Jack told me you're still single like me. Are you dating anyone seriously?"

"No." At this moment, Catherine could honestly answer no. "Are you?" She had to ask. It was like probing a sore tooth, but she felt compelled to hear the words.

"No. My last serious relationship ended about six months ago. Then a while back, I met David Britton while I was looking for you."

Her eyes glistened with unshed tears. "I fell so hard for him. He's the most wonderful man I've ever known. We had one date, but then he never called me again, except for business reasons." Her voice quavered. "He says he's getting married to someone else."

More tears ran from the corners of her eyes. "I'm still trying to understand how he could have met and fallen in love with someone else so fast. Maybe if I tell you about it, you can help me figure out what I did wrong. I know he liked me at first. That's what—"

There was a tap on the door and Jack and David came into the room carrying cups of hot coffee.

Catherine jumped from her chair. She wanted to run and keep on running, but she knew she couldn't.

David had begged Catherine to let him tell Shannon the truth before the two women met. Catherine had refused to consider it.

That had been a terrible mistake. Now Shannon was confiding something painful and private to her, the way sisters did. Heavens! They *were* sisters. The proof lay before Catherine's eyes.

She couldn't possibly tell Shannon about her and David now. His gaze searched Catherine's as he handed her a cup, but she looked away.

Jack sidled close. "Do you want us to leave?" he asked.

She shook her head.

"Hey, Shannon, did CC tell you she designed the renovation for the Crompton warehouse where you had dinner?" Jack leaned comfortably against David's desk.

No. Don't bring that up.

"Actually," Catherine said quickly, "Shannon told me she's been offered a prestigious job at a hospital here in Portland." At that revelation David shot Catherine an enigmatic glance. "Which one did you say it was, Shannon?"

"I don't think I mentioned it. It's Sacred Heart."

"I've been in there a few times."

Shannon stared at Jack with concern. "Why?"

"I guess CC didn't get around to bragging about me yet."

"Jack is Oregon's foremost race car driver," David said. "One day he'll probably win the Indianapolis 500."

"I thought your brother, Mitch, was headed in that direction."

David gave a careless shrug of his shoulders.

"He's dropping the racing circuit to go to graduate school."

"CC?" Jack began, almost too casually. "While we were in the coffee shop, you had a message on your cell phone. You've got a client, Mr. Ray, waiting for you at your office. I guess it's some kind of emergency so you'd better deal with it right now.

"I have to drive over to the track in a few minutes to see the guys about my race next week. Why don't you go with me, Shannon? We'll pick up my girlfriend, Melanie, on the way. Later on, I'll bring you back here to get your car."

"I can drop you at your office on my way home," David offered quietly.

Catherine stood in a kind of stupor while she finished her coffee. There *was* no Mr. Ray. Something was going on. David must have sensed she needed an escape; obviously he and Jack had concocted this excuse. But she also knew Shannon was expecting something of her.

"I'm sorry, Shannon. I had no idea we'd be interrupted like this. Why don't you go with my brother and Melanie? I promise you'll have a great time." She reached in her purse. "Here. This is my business card. I have your number now. We'll call each other and get together for lunch next week."

Catherine could tell that Shannon wished they were meeting sooner. But all she said was, "That sounds wonderful."

"Come on, Shannon. The guys in the crew are

going to think you're Catherine. It ought to be very amusing.''

''Just don't leave Shannon alone with Phil.''

''Phil's my best friend.''

''He's a terrible tease.'' There was a time when Catherine had been very attracted to Jack's partner. Phil was divorced and he'd had several subsequent relationships; as a result, she'd been a little frightened by his experience with women. But although Phil had flirted with her, he'd never actually asked her out.

''Never fear, Shannon. You'd be safe with him,'' Jack assured her.

''Well, all right, then.'' She turned to Catherine. ''I'll see you next week.''

Catherine nodded. She probably should have shaken her hand or kissed her cheek, but for some reason she couldn't seem to move.

Shannon lifted her eyes to David. Catherine couldn't watch. ''Thank you for letting us meet here.''

''It was my pleasure.''

Shannon followed Jack out the door.

David shut it with his foot.

''I could tell this was very hard on you,'' he said. ''After talking it over with Jack, I thought it would be wise to cut this first meeting short. Shannon is a force to contend with. Right now, a little goes a long way.''

She sucked in her breath. ''I'm glad you intervened. Th-there's something I have to tell you.''

"Do you want to talk here, or shall we do it in the car?"

"Here, and then I'll call a taxi."

"I said I'd drive you home. That's what I intend to do. Let's go. We can talk on the way."

His no-nonsense tone propelled her out the door. Afraid he might touch her, Catherine made sure she kept enough distance between them. The last thing she wanted was to have Shannon catch a glimpse of them and think they looked like a couple.

Once inside his car, he gave her a frank stare. "How long do you plan to allow this deception to continue?"

Averting her eyes, she lowered her head. "She's so nice, David. You can tell she's lost everything. I admire her for being able to function the way she does without family, without anyone.

"With her brains she could have been a doctor, but she chose nursing. It's probably the hardest kind of work there is, the hardest kind of service a person can render. That's what she's given her life to."

David said nothing.

"She didn't barge in on me," Catherine said after a while. "Even though I know there was so much more she wanted, she was careful not to rush me." The tears began to flow. "She's such a *good* person."

Catherine leaned her head back suddenly, and a self-deprecating laugh escaped. "I was so worried about what she'd be like. What her life might be like. She's so different than I'd imagined.

"I wish I had more of her qualities. Without my family for support, I'd be a total disaster. I know it.

"Dad had the money to build us a luxurious home, take us on exotic vacations, send me away to graduate school. Her father didn't make enough money to allow them to adopt another baby.

"She had to hold down a part-time job and work hard to get through graduate school, and she had to make it on her own. She nursed her mother through a lingering illness." Catherine turned to him. "Who helps Shannon when she's feeling down? How does she handle being alone in the world?"

With both hands she wiped the moisture off her cheeks. "She'll be a big hit with Jack's friends. Shannon has a sweetness in her that I don't have. I'm a willful, selfish, self-centered, spoiled woman who never had to work for anything in my life. It was all handed to me on a silver platter.

"Perfect parents, perfect brothers, a perfect home. Friends, acceptance. Exposure to the world. A wonderful career. The good life.

"Of the two of us, she's definitely the better person." Her voice trembled, and she shook her head. "No wonder you were so attracted to her. She's lovely and kind. There's a naïveté about her that's very endearing. Do you know she thinks you're the most wonderful man she's ever met?"

Still without saying anything, David started the car. Soon they'd reached the street and were on their way to her condo.

"When you walked in on us just now, she was

telling me about her evening with you. She opened up to me so naturally, it was as if we'd been best friends all our lives. The only way I can describe it is what I've seen among some of my friends and their siblings. A sister-to-sister kind of thing.

"She wanted help figuring out why you never called her for another date. You should have seen the bewilderment in her eyes, heard the pain in her voice. She was so sure you'd liked her in the beginning. She hoped I could tell her what she'd done wrong to explain why you suddenly lost interest.

"The strange thing is, I don't see anything about her not to like. But she's been hurt, David. The last thing I want to do is hurt her anymore. I couldn't bear to have that on my conscience."

"So what are you saying?"

He pulled into the guest parking space of her condo and shut off the engine.

"I—I'm not going to tell her about us."

A river of broken ice carved a deep channel through David's heart. He knew where her conversation was leading. His mother's insights had given him the knowledge to deal with moments like this. But the masochistic side of himself still had to hear the words.

"So where does that leave you and me?"

"There can't be a you and me," she said in a low voice. "I'm not going to see you again."

"Just like that. It doesn't matter about my feelings." His anger flared suddenly.

"Our feelings don't count here. You could have any woman you want, and we both know it."

"I want you."

"*She* wanted you first. If she can't have you, I can't have you, either."

"Even if you're in love with me?"

"That's not the point."

"Then we all lose."

"That's what sacrifice is about. It's past time I learned the meaning of the word."

"This person you think is so wonderful—you don't give her much credit, do you."

"For what?"

"Do you honestly believe she'd be happy if she knew that in her quest to find her sister, she would end up causing us untold grief and pain?"

"If we stop seeing each other, it's a moot point. In Shannon's case, ignorance is bliss."

"No, Catherine. There will be no bliss. Not for anyone involved. What you're proposing is totally dishonest to her, to you and to me.

"The other day you used the word 'wrong.' The only wrong I see is not allowing her to use her brains and compassion to handle the truth."

When Catherine turned to him, her face was drawn, her mouth taut. "Shannon's my identical twin, not yours. She's fragile. Believe me, if she had any idea I was the woman you loved, it would destroy her. And that would destroy me." Her voice trailed off.

*If Catherine discovers that her life was better than
Shannon's, then she'll feel guilty....*

"I can't be your architect, David. There will be
no charge for the work I've done. There wouldn't
have been a charge, anyway. As you know, it's been
a labor of love," she whispered. "Just go ahead and
throw away anything I've given you."

"You mean like the ring, along with all the memories and our future dreams?"

"David—please don't make this any harder than
it is."

He fought to control his rage over an impossible
situation. "Have you considered I might be fragile,
too? Did it ever occur to you that in ending our
relationship, you could destroy *my* life?"

She wrung her hands. "I don't believe that.
You're too strong a person."

"How do you know what I am? Don't let my
being a man fool you, Catherine. You and I belong
together. There won't be another life for either of
us!

"I realize you don't want to hurt Shannon, so let
me be the one to break the news to her. I'll tell her
you were willing to sacrifice our love in order not
to hurt her, but I forced the issue."

"No, David! Finding me should be a happy experience for her. Instead, she'll feel betrayed by her
own twin and wish she'd never begun her search.

"Don't you see what will happen? She'll quietly
fade into the background rather than intrude. I can

picture her going back to her lonely existence. She'll be in so much pain—and who will she turn to?''

David had never felt so helpless in his life. "You're internalizing all this, Catherine. You're projecting what *you* imagine you'd be thinking if you were Shannon. But you aren't the same person! She's lived twenty-eight years without you. She has a life!''

"What life? She's alone.''

David raked an unsteady hand through his hair. "Only in your mind, Catherine. She has friends, colleagues…. How can I make you see this objectively?''

"There's no way to be objective when it comes to damaging your twin sister!'' she blurted, then broke down sobbing. When she'd recovered enough to talk, she said, "But I have the power to remedy that situation.''

"What are you talking about?''

"She's been trying to get a job here in Portland. When you rejected her for a position at your clinic, she applied for a head nursing position at Sacred Heart Hospital. It's hers for the taking, if she wants it. She did all this to be near me.''

No, Catherine. She did it to get close to me.

"If she decides to accept the position, then she'll need a place to live. The next time I see her, I'm going to tell her she can move in with me. I'm the only family she's got. She can sleep in my spare bedroom.''

"It's really true, isn't it?'' he said dully. "Blood

is thicker than water. I can see you've worked everything out and you don't need me anymore.''

His mother had talked about his ability to cope. But it was no longer a question of coping. How did he cope when Catherine had left him with absolutely nothing?

He got out of the car to open the passenger door; fearful of touching her, he kept his distance. ''For what it's worth, I wish you and Shannon the joy of each other. Goodbye, Catherine.''

David had no idea what to do next. But if he hesitated, it meant he hadn't learned a thing and was willing to subject himself to more of the same punishment.

Running on adrenaline, he got in the car and turned out of the drive to merge with the traffic. He didn't watch through the rearview mirror to see if she was still standing there.

CHAPTER ELEVEN

HE'S GONE, CATHERINE. He's out of your life.

With a sense of unreality, Catherine entered her apartment. Her gaze darted to the dining room table, where she'd left some of the drawings for his new office complex. There were more drawings in the spare bedroom.

The roses he'd sent her stood in the vase, but their heads had started to droop. Several photos she'd taken of him with the camera she carried in her purse stared at her from the refrigerator.

Every shred of evidence would have to be thrown out before she could allow Shannon in the condo. Without wasting a second, she found a large plastic garbage bag and tossed everything inside. Even the photos in her wallet. In a state of frenzy, she hurried outside the building to dump the bag in the waste disposal bin.

On her return, she changed into jeans and a T-shirt, then began dismantling her drafting table. Within an hour, she'd set it up in the living room by the windows, where there would be plenty of light. In another hour, she'd removed everything from the spare bedroom, leaving it spotless for her sister.

While she sat on the couch sorting through the things she'd taken out of the other room, Jack and Melanie appeared at the door. Jack paused midstride to see her drafting table at the end of the room.

"What's going on?"

"I'm getting the spare room ready for Shannon to move in."

"I don't recall her mentioning anything about that to us."

"She doesn't know. I'm going to call her tonight and invite her to live with me. If she'd like to start moving in tomorrow, I want to be ready."

His brows met in a frown. "This is awfully sudden, isn't it?"

"She's been looking for me for a year, and I don't want her to have to wait any longer. Do you know her plans? Was she going to drive back to Tacoma tonight, or is she staying in Portland until tomorrow?"

"As far as I know, she intended to head home first thing in the morning," Melanie explained.

"Did she tell you the name of her hotel?"

"No, but David probably knows."

She averted her eyes. "I can't ask him."

"Why not?"

"Because it's over between us. Over for good."

"Just like that?"

A few hours ago, David had said those same words to her.

"I don't want to talk about him. Not ever again."

"Did you two have a fight?"

"No. He isn't that kind of man. When I explained I couldn't see him anymore because I couldn't hurt my sister like that, he understood we have to make sacrifices. He helped me from the car, wished me and Shannon the joy of each other and left."

"What about the complex you're designing for him?"

"He's going to find another architect. I've already got rid of everything so Shannon will never know of my connection to him. Tell me what happened when you went to the speedway with her."

"Well, for one thing, we bumped into Mitch Britton while we were there. He thought Shannon was you."

Her head jerked around in fear. "Did he give anything away about me and David?"

"Yes."

Her body went rigid. "What exactly did he say?"

"Before I could introduce either of them, he hugged her hard and begged her to make it right with his brother because the man was going through hell."

"Oh, no!"

"At that point I broke in and told him Shannon was your twin sister. I covered by saying that every guy at the track was in love with you. Mitch was so stunned, he played along. I don't think anyone actually said his name."

"Don't worry," Melanie reassured her. "Shannon laughed with the pit crew over the remark, and of course, Phil flirted outrageously with her. If she gave Mitch's comment any more thought, it didn't show.''

''I'd forgotten Mitch might be there,'' Catherine said in a shaking voice.

''As you're going to find out in the days ahead, it'll be damn well impossible to hide all traces of your relationship with David from her, CC. You'd better come clean the next time you see her, before another slip occurs that can't be fixed as easily.''

''There won't be any more slips. David and I haven't known each other that long. We've kept to ourselves. There's no reason to believe anything else could happen.''

''Don't be so sure. Shannon's no dummy, CC. She's as smart as you are.''

''Do you like her?''

They both nodded.

''I thought so. She likes you, too. When you told her you were taking her to the track, she didn't hesitate.''

''David told me not to give her a choice. As I've been saying, he's hurting like crazy, CC. He deserved some time alone with you.''

''Well, that's all over now.''

''All the guy did was tell you the truth so there'd be no unpleasant surprises. I never dreamed his honesty would rebound like this. What you're doing to him is cruel.''

Catherine swung around. ''It's a case of *not* being cruel to Shannon. I never thought I'd like her as much as I do. She needs protecting.''

''From what? She's a strong woman, just like you!''

''There's a vulnerability about her that makes me want to take her in my arms and tell her everything's going to be all right.''

''How come you insist on seeing her as something she's not? Her parents doted on her. After her mother died, she was left the family home and enough insurance to live comfortably. A group of her unmarried girlfriends travel together. She's been to the Orient and South America with them. She's worked in Alaska.

''I found out she's a lot more experienced than you are when it comes to men. She's been seriously involved with three guys, and lived with one for a year, hoping it would end in marriage. Eventually, he admitted he didn't want children and she did, so they broke up.

''She's a looker, just like you. Phil got her phone number already. He wants to take her out to dinner. There's nothing about Shannon's life to feel sorry for!''

''You don't understand, Jack. Without her saying anything, I felt certain emotions coming from her. Hidden emotions. Maybe it's the twin bond I've always heard about. All I know is, now that we've met, I can tell she needs me desperately.''

''No. David Britton is the person who wants and needs you desperately. I hope you wake up soon and realize it.'' He put his arm around Melanie. ''We've got to go. Take care.''

The second they went out the door, the phone began to ring. It might be a client. She would listen to the message, then go for a drive to clear her head.

"Hello, Catherine? It's Shannon. I just had to call and tell you how much today meant to me. I'll never be able to put it into words, but I'm so grateful you were kind enough to meet me when I knew you didn't want to.

"When David called and said you were willing to see me, I knew in my heart you were a very kind person. Much kinder than I am. I'm awfully willful at times. If the shoe had been on the other foot and I'd been the one who didn't want to be found, I might have let things go unresolved for a long time, maybe forever.

"Not you. You faced me. I have to admit I'm jealous. David said that twins have all kinds of hang-ups that might prevent us from getting together. The next time I talk to him, I'll have to tell him that of the two of us, you're definitely the better person.

"I envy you for having brothers. Jack and Melanie took perfect care of me today. I've got to think of a special way to thank them, and I'm counting on you for help in that department.

"Well, I know this is a long message. If by any chance you get home and want to call me tonight, I'm staying at the Brookshire Inn downtown, room fourteen eleven. Otherwise, if I don't hear from you, I guess we'll talk next week. I can't wait. There's so much I want to ask you, I hardly know where to start.

"Oh, and judging by the reception I got at the speedway today, it's clear you have a host of male admirers. I'm thrilled my sister is held in such high regard by everyone. Since you seem to have a way with men, maybe you could share your tips with me. If it's not too late, I'd like to salvage my relationship with David.

"Listen to me go on and on. I told you I was going to end this message, and I will. Just want you to know I love you already." The answering machine clicked off.

"Ms. CASEY?"

"Yes, Janine?" she answered a little too tersely. It was only nine o'clock on a Thursday morning. Already Catherine had another gigantic headache. She hated to admit it, but after living with Shannon for close to two weeks, headaches had become part of her daily burden.

In her heart of hearts, Catherine feared her headaches had started because she'd been trying without success to blot David from her consciousness. Every time Shannon brought his name into the conversation, Catherine told her she couldn't help out when it came to advice about men. Then she changed the subject.

In an effort to make certain David never became a topic of discussion, Catherine thought up activities to keep them too busy for private chitchat. One way to do that was to drive to her parents' home. They'd gone there every day after work and stayed until ten or later.

They'd spent the previous weekend there, too. The entire family had managed to convene. They made Shannon feel like one of them. Jack's crew also helped entertain her while they worked on his car.

Shannon had enjoyed it all so much, she hadn't been able to stop talking—about the Casey family, the house, each individual member of the crew, what various people had said to her...anything and everything. Catherine found she couldn't wait to get to the office every morning in order to snatch some breathing space for herself.

"I made a huge faux pas just now and I hope you'll forgive me," Janine was saying.

Her secretary made so many of them, Catherine had lost count. But Janine was cheerful and easy to work with, two traits Catherine prized in a secretary. In time she would grow into a capable assistant, or so Catherine hoped.

"Of course, Janine. What's the problem?"

In a hushed voice she said, "I didn't know you had a twin sister. When she came in, I thought it was you! I figured that you'd slipped out the rear door and you were returning. I think it made her mad."

Shannon was in reception? Why wasn't she at work?

Catherine had to force herself not to erupt. "If my sister's upset, then it's directed at me," she said in a soothing voice. ''I was planning to bring her here one day and introduce her to everyone, but it appears she's beaten me to it. Send her in.''

That was a problem of Shannon's. She was *always* beating Catherine to it. Whatever it was, she was invariably one step ahead. Shannon's methodical brain was driving Catherine crazy. She didn't know how much longer they could live together without there being some kind of explosion.

''Surprise!''

''Hi, Shannon. You gave my secretary a jolt!''

''I know. I didn't mean to.''

''I realize that. You and I have been so busy getting acquainted with each other, I'm afraid I haven't gotten around to letting other people know about you yet.

''Anyway…what are you doing here? When I left home, I thought you were getting ready to go to the hospital.''

''I called and said I'd be in late.''

Catherine frowned. ''Is anything wrong?''

''No. But I want to do something, and I'm afraid to try it alone.''

''What's that?''

''I gave everyone who helped us get together a gift. But I still haven't given David his. I thought maybe you could take an early lunch and go over to his office with me.''

''Not today,'' Catherine blurted in panic. ''I'm due at a new site in a few minutes.''

''You don't think it's a good idea, do you.''

"Do you want the truth?" she asked with pounding heart.

"Of course."

"No. I think it's a bad one."

"That's why you always change the subject when I want to talk about him, isn't it? You don't think there's any hope for me."

Beneath her desk, Catherine's legs trembled. "I think that when a man doesn't show interest in a woman after a first date, you have to accept the fact that nothing is going to happen. If it hadn't been for all of my brothers' insights, I probably would have made that mistake many times in my life."

Tears filled Shannon's eyes. "How do I get over him, then?"

Dear God. If I knew the answer to that question…

"I—I guess by meeting someone else. Why don't you return Phil's call and go out with him?"

She shook her head. "If you were never interested in him, then I'm sure I wouldn't be."

"Actually, at one time I was. Very interested, I mean. Let's face it. Most women find him nature's gift."

"What happened?"

"I learned he'd been married and divorced. It frightened me."

"Why?"

"Because I felt like he knew too much about women, about life. Sometimes he tried to psychoanalyze me. I hated that. One day he made me really angry."

"What happened?"

"During one of our verbal skirmishes in the garage, he said I must have had a bad experience with a guy and that's why I was so prickly. Of course, it *was* the truth, but I'd never let him know it.

"He had this ability to push all the right buttons and get a rise out of me every time he opened his mouth. At the time, I was a lot younger and too immature to handle a man like him.

"But you talk to any of the crew today and they'll tell you he's the greatest. Jack says there's a lot about Phil that nobody knows. He idolizes the guy."

"Really?"

"I'd love to see Phil try to take you on. We might look alike, but you could outpsychoanalyze him any day of the week."

"You think so?"

"Shannon, you intrigued him enough that he called you for a date. If you want to know the truth, he never asked me out. He just talked about doing it. With hindsight, I can see that I didn't challenge him."

"If I did decide to go out with him, he'd probably lose interest like David did. I couldn't bear that."

Catherine groaned inwardly. "Maybe you won't be interested in him, either."

"I have no idea. I have to admit he's attractive."

"Keep in mind Phil's been through a divorce. It's possible that his fear of a relationship not working out is greater than yours. Now, I really have to cut this short because I'm late for the site."

It was a lie, but she had to escape. When Shannon had mentioned going to David's office, Catherine hadn't been able to think about anything else. She wanted to be with him again so badly, she felt as though she was dying inside.

"Under the circumstances, I might as well go to work. I guess I'll see you around six."

They gave each other a hug, then left the office for the underground car park. Whenever they were seen together in public, heads turned, and today was no exception. It was a phenomenon Catherine wondered if she would ever get used to.

After waving Shannon off, she drove toward Cedar Hills. It was weeks since she'd been to David's property. But this morning the need to be close to him in any way at all dominated her thoughts and feelings.

Maybe he'd found someone else to design him a building and construction had already begun. If that was the case, she would know he'd moved on without her. Though terrified, she had to find out.

When the property came into view, she let out the breath she'd been holding. Nothing had changed. Everything looked the same as before. She pulled over to the side of the road and parked the car.

Memories of their first picnic together flooded back, and she felt a pang of intense longing for David, for those innocent weeks of rapture.

She'd planned to walk around the site, but she hadn't expected this acute sense of loss. Overwhelmed, she couldn't stop the tears and didn't dare get out of the car in case anyone noticed.

Twenty minutes must have passed before she got hold of herself enough to start the car. Checking her rearview mirror for traffic, she gasped to discover a car directly behind her. A black sedan. A Mercedes. An unsmiling gaze encountered hers. *David.*

She didn't know how long he'd been sitting there watching her. Since she had no business being at Cedar Hills, he could be in no doubt over the reason for her presence.

Running on pure emotion, she sped down the street, praying he wouldn't follow. She thought of a dozen places she could go to get away from him. But there was only one where she'd be safe.

Unmindful of the speed limit, she headed for her condo, taking a different exit in an effort to lose him. For that reckless maneuver, which she'd seen Jack do a hundred times, she picked up a patrol car. *Damn, damn, damn.*

Forced to heed the siren, she pulled over to the side of the road. If David caught up with her now...

For once there was something more terrifying than the sight of a policeman walking to her car to give her a ticket. Heart in her throat, she kept watching for the Mercedes, hardly listening to the officer's lecture about weaving in and out of traffic.

After a mumbled apology she pressed on to her condo at a slower speed, afraid David would be waiting at every corner. To her intense relief, he was nowhere to be found. Obviously she'd lost him.

Shattered by the experience of seeing him again, she got out of her car. She had to lean against the fender for a minute while she waited for strength to come back to her limbs. But the sight of him had left her too shaken. By the time she reached her condo, she was near collapse and couldn't get inside fast enough.

Only the door didn't click shut behind her.

She whirled, then almost fainted. David's tall, powerful body blocked the doorway.

Her hands went out in front of her to stave him off. "No! You can't come in!"

But David was already in. He shut the door and started toward her.

"How did you know I was coming back here? How did you get in the building?"

"Does any of that matter? I'm here now."

"David—you have to leave!"

"I'm not about to ravish you. Not yet, anyway," he muttered. "I just need to hold you for a minute."

"Shannon lives with me!"

"You think I don't know that? But she's at work now."

Not waiting for her permission, he pulled her into his arms. "It's been too long, Catherine," he whispered into her hair, reveling in the feel of her body. "Don't lie to yourself or to me anymore. This morning we both went out to that site because we don't have a life without each other. Are you going to go on torturing us like this?"

Too impatient for her answer, he found her mouth

and began kissing her voraciously. Always before, he'd practiced restraint, but no longer. After such a lengthy period of deprivation, the taste of her mouth, the feel of her body, released all inhibitions. He didn't care if he was out of control. This morning at the property he'd been given proof of her love. Nothing else mattered.

"David!" She cried his name over and over, but each time sounded more feeble than the last, until he'd broken through her defenses. Then she was the one kissing him, leaving him breathless.

Without conscious thought, he picked her up. "Which bedroom is yours?" he murmured against her lips.

"The first one." Her reply was muffled.

Their mouths clung as he started across the living room toward the hallway. Needing this shared love, this passion, they were both slow to register the sound of a key in the lock. Catherine reacted before he did, tearing her lips from his.

Her eyes reflected horror. "Quick—put me down!"

As her feet touched the floor, the door began to open. By the time Shannon had come inside, holding a shopping bag, Catherine had managed to reach the kitchen.

"What are you doing home?" they asked simultaneously.

This wasn't the way David had envisioned the truth emerging. But there was no holding back the moment.

"Hello, Shannon."

She wheeled around. Her eyes lit up when she saw him. "David! I didn't know you were coming over. How wonderful to see you!"

"It looks like all three of us didn't want to be at work today."

Shannon shook her head. "This is amazing. I went to see Catherine earlier this morning to find out if she'd go to your office with me. I wanted to give you a little present for the part you played in helping us get together. But she had an appointment. Anyway, here it is."

David made no move to take it from her. "That was very thoughtful of you, Shannon, but I can't accept it. When you hear me out, you'll understand why."

Catherine was signalling frantically behind Shannon's back that he should leave. But he had no intention of doing so.

"Let's all go in the living room and sit down, shall we?"

"Something's wrong, isn't it?"

He rubbed the side of his jaw. "Not wrong, Shannon. But a talk between the three of us has been long overdue."

"Don't do this, David."

"I have to, Catherine." He refused to meet her terrified gaze and sat down opposite the couch where Shannon had positioned herself. Catherine hovered in the doorway.

"I'll never forgive you."

"That's a chance I'm prepared to take."

He thought she would bolt, but eventually she subsided into another chair.

"Shannon? Catherine is the woman I fell in love with, the woman I want to marry."

To Shannon's credit, she remained in place, too, but the light had left her eyes.

"Your sister prayed this moment would never come. She never wanted to hurt you. But this lie we've all been living is an insult to you. It's not fair to any of us to let the situation continue."

Shannon set the shopping bag on the floor at her feet. "So that's what your brother meant when he saw me at the track and told me you were going through hell. Jack took that moment to break in and inform him I was Catherine's twin."

David blinked. "You met Mitch?"

"We weren't formally introduced, but there's a strong resemblance between you. I knew your brother was a race car driver, so I put two and two together. But there was so much joking going on with all the crew and drivers around, I didn't put any particular stock in his remark."

Mitch had kept that little piece of information from David. No doubt he hadn't wanted to tell him something that could have alarmed him further.

"So you've suspected this all along—about Catherine and me?"

"No. It wasn't until today that I began to wonder. Catherine's refusal to go to your office made me question why she was so quick to say no. It led me to think about other small instances that by themselves didn't mean anything. But putting them together—''

"You guessed the truth." He finished the sentence for her. "I'm sorry it's taken this long for everything to come out, Shannon. In fact, if Catherine had her way, it would never have come out.

"A little over two weeks ago we were engaged to be married. But once she'd met you, her fear of hurting you was so great, she gave me back the ring and said goodbye.

"Today we met by accident at some property of mine. Before she broke our engagement, she had agreed to be my architect for a new office complex to house the institute. But those plans were scuttled, too. When I saw her at Cedar Hills, I realized she was missing me as much as I've missed her. I followed her home to talk to her. That's when you came in.

"This wasn't a planned meeting. But since you're here, Shannon, you deserve an accounting. Catherine knows everything about the date you and I went on, the kiss I gave you outside the door of your hotel room. She knows that a few weeks later, I told you I was in love with another woman and planned to be married.

"At this point, there are no more secrets and I would like to hope we can all move forward. However, there is one thing I want you to know before I leave you both alone.''

At this point Catherine's and Shannon's heads

were bowed in exactly the same position, their hands clasped in exactly the same manner. The two sisters were so different—mentally, emotionally and psychologically—it took this frozen fragment of time to remind him that their bodies were still mirror images of each other.

"Both of you know my mother is a twin. When I told her about my broken engagement and the reason for it, we discussed the problems that arise between identical twins. She warned me that the two of you are very complicated human beings. Much more complex and intuitive than other siblings.

"She talked about fears. All people are plagued by them. It's part of the human condition. But Mother says identical twins carry around additional fears, which have to do strictly with each other.

"Being separated from birth made your experiences completely different, thus complicating your situation even more."

By now, both heads had lifted. Though Catherine wouldn't look at him, David could swear she was listening.

"I know there's a big question in your minds as to why I was attracted to both of you, but fell in love with Catherine. I wish there was a simple explanation for the connection between two people. Why it's there with one person, but not the other.

"I hope you're beginning to understand that in this affair we were all innocent. No one deliberately set out to be cruel to the other person. Another dynamic, much bigger and more complicated than the three of us could imagine, has been at work here. There's no place for blame.

"Having said that, I can't forget what Mother told me about the pain she went through with her twin sister. You share an intricate bond, and you're both hurting now. That's something no one can fix, only time.

"Mother's twin went to live in another part of the U.S. years ago. She couldn't have children, while Mother could. She held it against my mother. As a result, they've been apart for close to forty years.

"The separation is still hard on Mother. She loves her sister. I hope the same thing isn't going to happen to the two of you. I hope you can get past this moment, resolve these feelings. Nothing is important enough to destroy the love between two sisters who've been miraculously united. I happen to believe you need each other very much.

"So, no matter what my wants and needs are, I'm going to bow out. When I leave in a few minutes, neither of you will see me again, unless it's by accident.

"Don't get up. I'll let myself out."

CHAPTER TWELVE

IN A FEW STEPS David had left the building by the back stairs. The second he slid behind the wheel of his car, he reached for his cell phone and started punching in digits.

Be there, Jack.

"Yeah?" Someone answered on the fourth ring. David didn't recognize the voice.

"If Jack Casey's there, I'd like to speak to him, please."

"Hey, Jack? Phone!"

He could hear the clank of metal in the background.

"Yeah? This is Jack."

"It's David."

"Hey—any luck yet?"

David had to stop and take a deep breath. "No. In fact, there's been a new development. I'm not in the best shape."

Not only had Catherine let him go without a struggle, once he'd started talking, she'd never looked at him.

"It's too long a story to tell you over the phone. Can you take a little time off from work right now?"

"Sure."

"Thanks, Jack."

"Want to take a drive?"

"You're reading my mind. I was thinking the ocean."

"Sounds good to me. I haven't been there in a while. Swing by the garage and we'll go in my Porsche. It's a beautiful day. I'll put the top down."

"You're a lifesaver."

"I only wish I could be. CC's put you through the wringer. I've never seen her like this in my life. Trying to figure out women is impossible."

"You've got that right."

"I thought everything was great with Melanie until lately. Now she has this crazy idea that we can't get married until I've built my formula one car and can pay a crew to man it.

"Hell—I don't even know if that's going to happen, but she's dug in her heels because she's afraid a wedding and babies might interfere with my career. I'm about ready to quit this racing thing altogether."

"No, don't do that, Jack. Have you ever wondered if maybe she's just saying that because she knows you're worried about Catherine?"

"What do you mean?"

"You and your sister have always been close. It's possible she doesn't think this is the best time to be talking about a happy future with you, while the situation between Catherine and me has our families upset."

"Man, that could be it!"

"Just a thought."

"But it makes a lot of sense, David. Especially after the conversation I had with Mom last night."

"What was that about?"

"Melanie's insistence that we wait to get a ring made me angrier than usual. Mom picked up on my bad mood, so I told her what was going on. She sounded surprised because just last month Melanie came to her and asked if she'd do the flowers for our wedding. Mom's a natural at it."

"I met your sister a little over a month ago, Jack. The time frame fits."

"You're right."

"I'll be there in ten minutes. We'll talk about it then."

It would be a relief to discuss someone else's problems for a while. Melanie and Jack were perfect for each other. She put his happiness above her own; he was willing to give up his racing dreams for her. Theirs would be a solid marriage.

Right now, David couldn't see how his problem with Catherine could be resolved. For her twin's happiness, Catherine had turned her back on David. She was willing to throw away the great love they shared because of some false idea that it would ease Shannon's pain.

"What took you so long?" Jack called to him from the front seat of his car, his face deadpan.

David smiled. "Traffic!"

He parked his Mercedes and climbed into the Porsche. Portland was enjoying a few days of hot summer weather between spells of rain, and he relished the sun on his face.

Jack turned to him. "How soon do you have to be back?"

"To be honest, I hadn't thought beyond finding you."

"That's fine with me. I'm in the mood to take a swim."

They headed west.

"So tell me about this new development that's made you look so grim."

"Shannon caught me with your sister at the condo a little while ago." After he explained what had happened, Jack whistled.

"Well, what do you know? The deed is finally done, no thanks to my crazy, mixed-up sister. Thank God for your courage! I'll bet CC didn't know what hit her."

"I left while they were both still sitting there in shock."

"I'd love to have been a fly on that wall. Listen, David—I realize you're feeling pretty bad, but let me tell you something. This is exactly what was needed to bring CC to her senses. Trust me."

David undid his tie and tossed it in the back. "I figured I didn't have anything to lose."

"Hey, you did the right thing. There's going to be some change—nothing will stay static now."

"I'm glad you have so much faith. I'm afraid I've lost mine," David muttered in a bleak voice. "Your sister despises me on all counts."

"She wishes she could. Her anger's going to pass."

"In the next life, perhaps."

"That's where you're wrong. CC's in love with you. In order to counter the effect you have on her, she deliberately sabotaged your relationship by asking Shannon to share the condo with her."

"I'd like to think that, Jack. But let's not forget she's a twin who's probably been missing her twin connection."

"I don't know about that. We've been a close family all our lives. She's had girlfriends, but she never seemed needy. Just the opposite, in fact."

"Maybe you're right."

Jack slanted him a glance. "I know I am. It's a joke around our house that the day CC met you, no one saw her again."

Those words were a balm to David's aching heart.

They drove the last five miles to the coast in companionable silence. When they came in view of the ocean, Jack continued on until they arrived at a turnout and could park.

By tacit agreement, they got out of the car and walked to the rock wall, where they could sit and watch the surf.

David followed the line of waves breaking into curls at intervals before they frothed and foamed onto shore. "If this were the old days, I'd kidnap your sister and take her to someplace where she'd have to stay put until she saw reason."

Jack grinned. "I'll grab Melanie and join you."

"If only it was that easy." He sighed. "I don't want to do anything that might exacerbate Catherine's fears."

"Fears about what?"

Maybe talking about this to the brother who had known Catherine all her life would help. Heaven knew, David was grasping for solutions from any source. Who better than Jack?

"Did I tell you my mother is a twin?"

Jack stared at him. "No! Uh-oh. When you and CC get married, that means you might have twins."

"If we do get together, I'm counting on it," David said. "Anyway, like you, I recently had a talk with my mother. According to her, identical twins are complicated creatures."

By the time David had explained everything, a half hour must have passed, with dozens of cars stopping to enjoy the view.

There was a lot to absorb. Leaving Jack to his thoughts, David wandered to the water. He removed his shoes and socks, rolled up his pants and began walking through the wet sand. Before long, Jack joined him.

They found a huge rock and hoisted themselves to the top. Following each ebb, the water swirled around the base, tossing up spray. David enjoyed feeling the cool droplets on his face.

"Your mom was right when she said you should believe in the power of your love. CC may have invited Shannon to live with her, but it's all a big front because, deep down, she's dying to be with you. Anyway, whether you dropped your bombshell or not, they weren't destined to remain roommates much longer.''

''Why do you say that?''

''Because they're as different as night and day,'' Jack theorized. ''I've been waiting for the newness to wear off. I'll bet they got on each other's nerves from day one.

''I already know Shannon's a perfectionist. CC's the opposite. If she's in a hurry, she leaves everything a mess. Her creative side keeps her from obsessing about the small stuff. In that regard, she's easy to get along with.

''Shannon, on the other hand, is high-maintenance. There will come a point when CC has to walk on eggshells to get along with her.''

In spite of his anguish, David chuckled. ''Even though I've told them I've bowed out of the picture, you think there'll be a parting of the ways?''

''Oh, yeah. Definitely. For one thing, Shannon's been an only child. She's spoiled but doesn't know it. CC's spoiled, too—since she was the only girl— but it's been in a different way.

''Another thing, Shannon is used to being in charge of other people. She's probably been over-compensating because her dad always dominated her mother. Shannon is determined that won't happen to her, therefore she runs the show.

''She's probably done too much of that with the guys she's dated and it turned them off. She has to fall for some guy who won't take any of her guff—

and who won't leave her, either. Somebody who gives as good as he gets. I think she may have met her match with Phil.

"Except for Dad, CC doesn't take well to authority. She runs according to her own dictates, no one else's." Jack let out a bark of laughter. "I'll bet the first time Shannon tried to manage her, the sparks flew.

"You know what's funny? CC had the idea that Shannon is this poor, lonely little creature without a friend in the world. I'm pretty sure she's already found out that Shannon can roll over you like a bulldozer.

"Mark my words. Now the truth about you and my sister is out, there's going to be double trouble in paradise."

"You're right about that," David muttered. "I promised Catherine I'd never tell Shannon."

"You and I both know that's one promise you should never have made. CC's all mixed up right now. So's Shannon. They don't know which way they're going—neither one of 'em. They both needed help. Today you gave it to them.

"All you have to do now is stand back and wait for the fallout. I predict you and CC will be back together before you know it."

David's eyes closed tightly. Listening to Jack was like inhaling a lungful of invigorating ocean air. It seemed to clear his mind and breathe new life into his tortured soul.

THE SILENCE in the condo had become unbearable. Catherine hadn't dared move, let alone speak. Shannon was still sitting there, her head bowed. When the phone rang, neither of them stirred.

Catherine heard the familiar static, then a male voice on the answering machine. "Hello, Shannon. It's Phil. I don't know when you get home from work, but I'm hoping you hear this message in time to go out to dinner with me tonight. Be brave and give me a call back on my cell phone. I promise you won't be sorry. Talk to you later." He clicked off.

Phil's call broke the stalemate for Catherine.

"Shannon?" she ventured in a small voice, tears streaming down her face. "I'm so sorry."

Shannon got up from the chair, her back to Catherine. "So am I."

Catherine wiped the tears away with her hands. "It's finished between David and me. Do you think we can put this whole experience behind us and start over again?"

Her sister turned around with an incredulous look on her face. "You're not serious!"

"Of course I am!" Catherine cried. "We'll make this a brand-new beginning."

"That would be impossible."

"Why?"

"Surely you don't need me to answer that question! If you'll give me a few days to find myself an apartment, I'll move out of here. It'll be better anyway. I don't have your flair for design, but at least my place will be mine. I'll be able to surround myself with my own things."

"I don't want you to go, Shannon. Please. I'll do anything to make this work."

She shook her head. "It could never work. He wants *you*, not me."

"But you heard him. We're never going to see each other again."

"Oh, please… Spare me the rhetoric. He chose you. I can see why. Let's face it—you've got the advantage over me.

"The thing is, I'm never going to forget that you both lied to me. I forgive you, I guess. But that doesn't mean I can live with what's happened.

"You didn't tell me the truth, and because of that, I changed jobs and moved down here. My parents' home is going to belong to someone else in another few weeks. I left my friends, my career, my life, everything, just to be with you. Little did I dream I'd find betrayal at the end of the road."

The words were bitter, and they scorched Catherine.

"It's funny, you know?" Shannon went on implacably. "After Mother told me I had a twin, I used to fantasize what it would be like to be united with a brother or sister. I assumed, oh, so naively, that if my twin existed, he or she would be the one person on earth I could trust, the one person who would never hurt me."

Catherine rushed toward her and put her hands on Shannon's arms. "You *can* trust me. I didn't want to hurt you. Don't you realize that? You've got to give me another chance. I love you. We're sisters!''

"You don't know the meaning of the word *love*." Shannon wrenched herself away. "When your brother talked to me that day, he told me not to wait for you to look me up. He *knew* you couldn't care less about me. You think I'm so stupid that I don't understand why you finally relented?

"You were curious to meet the woman David was attracted to first! *That's* the only reason we ever got together. And it didn't take him long to make up his mind which twin he wanted, did it?

"That elaborate explanation he came up with about fear was ludicrous. Why couldn't the coward just admit I don't have any sex appeal and you do?

"You have this incredible power over men. I know, because I went to the track with Jack and Melanie. For a few minutes I found out what it was like to be inside your skin. I learned how it felt to be Catherine Casey, the woman all those men fantasize about.

"Phil wanted you first, but you weren't interested. The only reason he's calling me is because I look like you. Half a loaf is better than none, right?

"Your brothers are crazy about you. And your dad—his eyes light up like neon signs when you walk into a room.

"Below that degree of yours hanging on the wall of his study, he's hung the Cossutta award you won at the Harvard Graduate School of Design. I understand it's given annually to the one student who shows the greatest promise.

"That's my sister, Catherine."

Catherine shuddered at the relentless anger in Shannon's voice. Before she could speak—not that she knew what to say—Shannon forged ahead.

"Is it any wonder David took one look at you and proposed? As long as we're being honest here, tell me the truth. Did he ask you to marry him before or after he slept with you? I only got as far as a kiss before he ran away from me as fast as he could."

Help me.

"Answer me, damn you!"

"Don't do this," Catherine begged. She felt so ill she wanted to die.

"Do what? Demand a little honesty? I think you owe me that after all your treachery."

Catherine's breathing had grown shallow. "We've never slept together," she whispered.

The shock on Shannon's face was more disturbing than her rage. "Don't tell me— Besides everything else about your picture-perfect life, you're a virgin, too? My dad adopted the wrong girl."

In a sudden rush of insight, Catherine said, "I thought you had a good relationship with your father."

Her face closed. "It might have been—*if* I'd been perfect like you. But I could never quite measure up, no matter how hard I tried. Pretty soon it didn't seem to matter what I did because it was never good enough."

She started for the door.

"Wait, Shannon!" Catherine cried in panic. "Where are you going?"

"It's none of your business."

"Please don't say that! Don't leave. I know you're in pain, but we have to talk this out."

"No, we don't. It's twenty-eight years too late. I was warned that getting together with you might not be a happy experience. I didn't want to believe it. It's the story of my life, you know—rushing in, only to find disappointment." Her white face was the last thing Catherine saw before Shannon disappeared from the condo.

Catherine felt a sorrow and helplessness that went beyond tears. Shannon needed to be with someone who loved her, but everyone she knew in Portland had betrayed her. Who could blame her for running away like a wounded animal?

Putting herself in her twin's place, Catherine imagined Shannon had gotten into her car and was driving around blindly, not knowing where to go or what to do.

Furious with David for destroying her sister's life, Catherine was determined to talk to him. She tried reaching him on his cell phone. When he didn't pick up, she grabbed her purse and left for his office. In breaking his promise not to say anything, he'd done the unforgivable.

No matter what my wants are, they're not important enough to destroy the love between two sisters who've been miraculously united.

How *dare* he stand there and blithely say those words, then announce they'd never see him again unless it was by accident? Well—that accident was going to happen a lot sooner than he'd anticipated.

Outraged by his behavior, she reached the institute as fast as possible and swept into the reception area. The secretary behind the desk eyed her with speculation.

"Mr. Britton's not here," she said before Catherine had a chance to say anything.

That did it! "Why don't you let me be the judge of that?"

She strode past the other woman and entered David's office without knocking.

He wasn't there!

She spun to find the woman at her heels. "Where is he?" Catherine demanded.

"He's gone for the day, Ms. White."

"But I'm sure he's told you where you can get hold of him. He was at my place all of one half hour ago—and my name's Ms. Casey. I'm not leaving until you tell me where he is."

"Oh! I thought you were your sister! If I could tell you where he is, I would. Don't you have his cell phone number?"

"Yes. But he's not answering."

"I'm sure he will as soon as he can."

"If you talk to David before I do, tell him I'm looking for him. Ask him to phone me immediately."

"Of course."

Full of adrenaline, she hurried to her car and decided to pay Mitch Britton a visit. On the evening David had taken her to her parents' place, he'd driven past his stock-trading office and pointed it out. She knew his brother still worked there.

The two of them had an extremely close relationship. Mitch would know where to find David. Maybe she could persuade him to let her inside his brother's home, where David would be unable to avoid her.

David had met Shannon first. His cruelty today had provoked this crisis. As far as Catherine was concerned, he owed it to Shannon to try to repair some of the damage. Her sister was still in love with him; she would listen to David. He was probably the only person who could get through to her and convince her to give Catherine another chance.

Once again she marched through a set of glass doors and approached the receptionist at the desk.

"I'd like to see Mitch Britton, please."

"I'm sorry. He's not in."

"Do you know where I can find him? This is an emergency."

"He had an appointment at the university today. I have no idea when he'll be back. I'll take your name and phone number. If he calls, I'll give him the information. That's the best I can do."

"No, thank you. May I look at a phone book?"

"Yes. Of course."

Giving her a puzzled frown, the receptionist rummaged in her desk and found it. Catherine turned to the *B*s. She suspected David was at his mother's.

There were five Brittons listed, none of them with the name David or Mitch. But there was a William Britton on Astor Circle. If she recalled correctly, William had been their father's name.

Catherine thanked the receptionist, then headed out. Determined to waylay David as soon as possible, she revved the MG's engine and set off for the Britton family home.

It turned out to be an attractive two-story colonial house in one of the well-established residential neighborhoods of Portland. But to her chagrin, there were no cars on the street in front or in the drive.

She supposed he could have hidden his Mercedes inside the two-car garage. The only way to find out was to walk to the front door and ring the bell.

Driven by her chaotic emotions, she got out of the car and hurried toward the house. Before she reached the porch, an attractive older woman happened to open the door to collect the mail.

Catherine knew it was his mother and drew to a standstill. Both her sons resembled her a great deal.

"Hello, Catherine."

The warmth in the older woman's eyes caught her off guard. "You know me?"

"Oh, my, yes. David gave me some pictures of the two of you." His mother sounded so kind. Catherine felt like a fool.

"I—I'm trying to find him. By any chance, would he be here?"

His mother shook her head slowly. "No. I haven't seen or talked to him in several days."

"I wonder where he is? An hour ago he came to my place. I thought he might have come here afterward."

"No. I'm sorry."

"I—I'm the one who should apologize for bursting in on you like this unannounced, Mrs. Britton, but it's vital I get in touch with him."

"Would you like to come in and visit for a few minutes? Maybe he'll call while you're here."

"Didn't David tell you we're not seeing each other anymore?"

"Yes. But I'd still enjoy talking to the only woman who ever captured his heart. He looked twenty years old again the day he told me he was getting married. A mother who loves her son as much as I love David doesn't forget a moment like that."

Catherine averted her eyes. "If he told you why we broke up, then you'll understand why I don't feel it would be a good idea to come in."

"I know about your twin sister, Shannon. David said he was going to tell her the truth about his love for you."

"Yes, well, he did that today. And now Shannon's the reason I'm here," she murmured. "She's been hurt so terribly, and someone needs to help her. No matter what's happened, I believe she'd still listen to David if he was willing to try to comfort her. She's in love with him."

"The problem is, my dear, David is in love with *you*. To do as you suggest would only compound her pain—and his. Your broken engagement has hurt him deeply." She paused, her expression sympathetic.

A moment later, she continued. "You have to understand one thing about my son. After living so many years with the fear that he might have been responsible for Michael's death, he's learned that keeping a secret was the worst thing he could have done. It robbed him of so much happiness growing up. But I have to say I've never admired his integrity more than at this moment."

The tremor in her voice caused Catherine to lift her head in query.

"In telling the truth, he lost you. I know it's a very tragic loss for him, especially now that I've met you in person and can see how lovely you are."

"Thank you," Catherine whispered. This meeting with his mother had shattered her.

"If I do hear from him, I'll tell him why you were here, but I can't promise anything."

"No. Of course not. Thank you for talking to me."

"Anytime." Her eyes, so reminiscent of David's, gazed at Catherine with too much tenderness. "It's strange, but the minute I saw your picture and the diamond ring he'd bought for you, I thought of you as my daughter-in-law, and we hadn't even met yet."

Catherine fought to suppress her tears.

I wanted to meet you, too. I wanted to be your daughter-in-law. But not at Shannon's expense.

"Goodbye, Mrs. Britton," she managed to say.

"Goodbye, Catherine."

She made it to the car, but as she pulled away from the curb, she broke into sobs.

David. David.

Once she'd arrived at her condo, she hid her face so that if she ran into any of the building's other residents, they wouldn't see her swollen eyes. There was no sign of Shannon's car.

No sooner had she walked in the door than her cell phone rang. When she answered it, she discovered it was Mitch Britton returning her call.

"Hello, Mitch? It's Catherine Casey."

"Hi, Catherine." He sounded like his usual friendly self.

"I'm looking for your brother, but he's nowhere to be found. I was wondering if you'd do me a favor. It's very important."

"Of course."

"Could you let me in his apartment so I can wait for him? There's something I have to talk to him about and he's not answering my calls."

"Sure. I'm on my way home from the university. I'll meet you in the lobby of his building in twenty minutes."

"Thank you, Mitch. I'm leaving now."

CHAPTER THIRTEEN

IT WAS TWILIGHT when Jack drove his Porsche to the garage where David's car was parked.

David got out of the passenger seat. "Thanks for being there for me, Jack. I needed that."

"So did I. Keep the faith." Jack clapped him on the shoulder and they both went their separate ways.

David climbed slowly into the Mercedes. Unable to bear the thought of his own company, he decided to head to Mitch's apartment. When his cell phone rang, he automatically answered it.

"Hey, David, guess what?" his brother cried excitedly.

"Mitch? I was just planning to come by your apartment."

"Don't do that."

"Why not?"

"Because there's a surprise waiting for you at yours."

His heart started to pound. "Catherine?"

"Yeah. She's been looking all over Portland for you and asked me to let her into your place to wait. I told her to meet me in the lobby."

"How soon will she be there?"

"She's probably already there."

Jack had prophesied that nothing would remain static.

He sucked in his breath. "I'll take over from here. Thanks, Mitch."

David drove as if his car had wings. Sure enough, when he entered his building's parking area, he saw her car in one of the guest spaces. Adrenaline charged his system. He leaped from the driver's seat, craving the sight of her.

"Catherine?" he said softly as he entered the lobby. For the moment they were alone. She'd been gazing out the other set of doors. At the sound of his voice, she whirled. One glance told him how anxious she was, how desperate.

He fought to keep his hands at his sides. "Mitch told me I'd find you here."

"I've been looking and calling everywhere for you." She was out of breath.

"Well, I'm here now. Let's go upstairs where it's private so we can talk."

"No, we don't have time!" she blurted. "Shannon's gone!"

"She probably needed to get away by herself."

David could tell Catherine was trembling. Her beautiful gray eyes glistened with tears.

"When I'm hurt, I have a family to go to. She has no one! I'm really worried about her, David. She left my place so heartbroken, you can't imagine. When I phoned the hospital, they said she'd called in sick. Mom and Dad haven't seen or heard from her. I just phoned Jack and he doesn't have a clue where she could be.''

His elation that Catherine had come to him made it almost impossible to remain calm, but somehow he had to contain his emotions.

"What would you like me to do?"

"Will you try to find her? Please? She loves you. Even though she's hurting, I have a feeling she'll listen to you."

"She's probably gone to Tacoma for the night."

"That's what I think. She has a friend, Amy Walsh. I called Amy's number several times, but no one answered. Still, she might get home later. I think it would be best if you went to her apartment and talked to her. Find out if she's heard from Shannon. I have her address."

"Even if I tracked Shannon down, what would you want me to say to her, darling?"

"Please don't call me that."

"How can I not? I'm in love with you. I always will be."

"David," she said in exasperation, "you're the only one who can convince Shannon that I really care about her, that I want us to start over. If she doesn't want to live with me, Mom and Dad have invited her to stay with them for as long as she wants. They think she's wonderful, and that would be a good solution for all of us. You could make her listen."

Maybe the gods were on his side, after all.

"You're right. It's a good idea."

"Thank you, David!"

"Don't thank me before you hear the condition."

"What?"

"I'm not stepping one inch from this lobby unless you come with me."

She shook her head. "I couldn't."

"Why not?" he demanded. "She already knows the truth about us."

"No. Don't ask me!" she begged.

"Catherine, darling, you're the only one who can extend her your parents' invitation."

It pleased him that she couldn't refute his statement.

She bit her lip. "After the speech you made about never seeing me or Shannon again unless it was by accident, how's she going to feel when she sees you and me together at Amy's door?"

"I suspect she'll forgive us when she realizes we cared enough about her welfare to come looking for her. Especially since we were concerned enough to drive all the way from Portland to Tacoma to make sure she's all right. That ought to give her a lot to think about."

Several people walked into the lobby, inhibiting Catherine from responding. Though it was a calculated risk, David took advantage of their presence.

In a voice the others could hear, he said, "Hold the elevator, please?" Then he turned to Catherine. "What will it be? The decision is yours."

Three different people who all lived in the building were watching them with uncommon interest.

He knew he'd put her in a difficult position. He could practically hear her working it out. If she refused to go to Tacoma with him, then he'd go upstairs, and that would be the end.

She hesitated so long he realized he'd underestimated her determination to stay away from him.

"So be it," he muttered, and started for the elevator.

"No—wait!" she called just as he entered and the doors began to close.

He wedged his foot in the opening and squeezed his way through. "Let's go, shall we?"

Without asking her permission, he caught her elbow and ushered her to his car. For the moment, it was enough just to be able to touch her like this.

The charged silence between them was nothing like the easy quiet on the drive with Jack earlier. Night had come to the Northwest. He turned on the headlights, which automatically lit up the dash. In the semidarkness he could study her profile to his heart's content.

Needing to touch her, he reached for her hand. She tried to pull away but he held on tightly until she let her hand relax in his. She still refused to look at him. That was all right. As long as there was this much physical contact, he wasn't going to complain. Not after two weeks of hell without her.

They passed the turnoff for Chehalis. Another hour to go. He switched on one of their favorite tapes. Rachmaninoff's *Theme on Paganini* took him back to a night they'd gone to the symphony, the second week he'd known her.

That was the night she'd turned to him during one of the most beautiful passages. It was the moment he'd been waiting for—the sense of unspoken commitment between them. It had been unmistakable. She couldn't possibly listen to this music and not remember.

He rubbed his thumb slowly against her palm. "I love you, Catherine."

She lowered her head.

"How bad was it after I left you alone with Shannon?"

"Bad," she whispered in a husky voice.

"It's always darkest before the dawn. That old cliché is as true now as the first time I heard it."

"What if we find her and make everything worse?"

"It couldn't get worse. There's only one way it can go from here."

She shivered. "I pray you're right."

"I know I am." He lifted her hand to kiss each finger. She was trembling. "I've missed you."

Her gasp resounded in the air. "Please, let's not talk anymore." She reached out to turn off the tape.

"You're exhausted. Why don't you sleep until we get to Tacoma?"

SHANNON SAT in Amy's kitchen, watching her make coffee. "You're so wonderful to put up with me, especially since you were on the night shift at Glen Cove. I know I've been awful company.''

''Hey, that's what friends are for. You've done the same thing for me plenty of times.''

''I should have listened to you when you told me to forget what Mom said about my being a twin. Then I would never have met David. I would never have quit my job and sold the house. Honestly, Amy, I don't think I've ever been in so much pain in my life.''

Her friend brought their mugs to the table and sat down. ''I realize it hurts, but two weeks ago you told me you suspected he and Catherine were an item.''

''I know. But it's one thing to think it, and another to walk in on them today and have him announce it point-blank!''

Amy sipped hot coffee. ''How would you have liked him to handle it?''

''As soon as David met Catherine at the speedway, he should have told me.''

''I thought you said that legally, he couldn't do that. By the time she decided to meet you, the two of them had fallen in love.''

''But he knew how much *I* loved him! That knowledge alone should have made him forget his damn rules and just tell me.''

''But he didn't know how you felt. How could he on the strength of one date? Anyway, speaking of rules, let me show you a little book I picked up the other day. It's in the bedroom.''

When she returned, she put it in front of Shannon. *Rules That Work. A Woman's Guide to Marriage.*

''I think we've read every word on the subject, Amy, and we're still single.''

''This one's different. I've studied it from cover to cover. The opening statement says, 'Love implies mutual reciprocity between two people. If that isn't your situation, then you're not in love.'

''That isn't what happened to you and David Britton. He was attracted enough to take you out to dinner and kiss you good-night. But that was the end of it. He never led you on, he never took you out again or accepted any invitations from you. Which means you couldn't have been in love with him! You were infatuated with him.

''According to the author, infatuation has nothing to do with love. It's a phenomenon that goes on in one person's head only. It's a fantasy. It has nothing to do with anyone else. An infatuated person is like a teenager who thinks she's fallen in love with a rock star she's never met and never will. It's all in the mind. It's fiction.''

Shannon finished her coffee. ''I don't think I can take this tonight, Amy.''

''I'm not trying to hurt you. But, Shannon, I recognize myself on every page of this book. At thirty years of age, I think I'm finally starting to see what I've been doing wrong all this time. Remember that thing I had for Stewart?''

Shannon nodded.

''After I read this part about infatuation, I felt like

an idiot. I wasted a whole year on him. For nothing!''

''Multiply that by a hundred and you'll know how I felt today. I couldn't stand being in the same room with her, so I left the condo and drove here as fast as I could.''

Amy put some doughnuts on the table.

''I know she's an architect, but what's she *really* like?''

''She's everything I'm not.''

''Oh, for heaven's sake, Shannon. Of course you two are different! You grew up apart. You may have identical bodies, but you have your own spirits, your own talents, your own virtues and flaws. Do you like her?''

''I did.''

''Until…''

''Until I found out she was planning to marry the man I love.''

''I thought we'd already established that it isn't love you feel for David Britton.''

''No. *You* did.''

''I know it's been awful, but from what you've told me, they never intentionally tried to hurt you, and they've even broken their engagement.''

''That's not going to last more than five minutes.''

''Then it means they're in love, because what they share is mutual and it isn't fantasy. They're living the reality. That's what I want for both of us.''

They looked at each other, and Shannon nodded wordlessly.

"Your sister sounds like a nice person. She didn't want to meet you at first but still took the risk. He sounds nice, too, Shannon. In the end, he told you the truth at the cost of having to give up the woman he loves."

Shannon stared at her friend. "I thought you were on my side."

"I am, but after reading this book I can see how skewed some of my ideas about love have been. Analyze what really happened to you—what you'll see is that there is no enemy.

"You should read chapter ten. It talks about the difference between hurt pride and a broken heart. Pride screams for revenge. Remember how I never gave Stewart those phone messages from his girlfriend in order to get back at him for not being interested in me?"

"Yes."

"That's revenge."

"I'm not planning to do anything like that."

"Maybe not consciously. But if you stay mad at your sister, you'll keep apart two people who love each other. That's pretty sad, considering you've been looking for your twin for a whole year."

"How am I supposed to be close to her when she's going to marry David?"

"Read chapter five. It's called Moving On."

"That's a lot easier said than done."

"I know. I'm living proof. But it would be sad if

it took you as long as it took me to get over a man who was never in love with me. Let me read what the last paragraph of the book says.

"There is only one prince per pond. Fortunately, there are millions of ponds each with its own prince. Out of those millions, there are at least twenty princes who were meant for you. Continue your search till you find the one who reciprocates your feelings. Don't settle for anything less."

Amy put the book down. "I've done a lot of settling since my twenties."

"Tell me about it," Shannon murmured grudgingly.

She heard the doorbell. "Don't let anyone in, Amy."

"Don't worry, I won't."

While she waited, Shannon poured herself another cup of coffee.

"Shannon? David and Catherine are at the front door. They've been looking all over for you and they're very relieved to find out you're spending the night with me. If you don't want to talk to them, they understand and they'll go. But they had to make sure you were all right. What do you want me to tell them?"

Shannon stared blindly out the kitchen window. "I can't see them right now. I'm too upset."

"Okay. Is there any other message?"

"No."

Amy wasn't gone long. When she rejoined Shannon, she said, "They left. But before I shut the door, Catherine told me to tell you she loves you."

As Amy's arm went around her, Shannon broke down sobbing.

WHILE CATHERINE STOOD beneath the porch light of Army's apartment, face buried in her hands, David gathered her in his arms. He kissed her hair. "We have to give her time," he whispered. "She's probably been crying her eyes out and doesn't feel up to seeing anyone right now. Come on, Catherine. Let's go home."

He put his arm around her shoulders and led her to the car, which he'd parked outside the duplex. When they'd driven beyond the outskirts of Tacoma, he felt her stir.

"I'm sorry, David."

"For what?"

"I should never have asked you to come here in the first place. It was a fool's errand."

"Not at all. No matter how hurt Shannon may feel, she now has proof that we weren't off somewhere else enjoying ourselves at her expense. She'll realize this isn't a happy time for any of us.

"Before we arrived, she probably envisioned all kinds of things. But I'm sure our presence here has dispelled the negative ones.

"What's important is that we know she's spending the night with a good friend. You were worried about her being alone. As you can see, she does have a support system. That's what you wanted to find out, isn't it?''

"Yes.''

"If you'd been in her shoes, I doubt you would have come to the door, either. But maybe there's something else you can do.''

"What's that?''

"Would you like to use my cell phone and call Amy's? She probably won't answer, but you could leave a message. Tell her all the things you wanted to say to her face.''

"I—I don't dare phone her this late.'' But she didn't seem averse to the idea.

"It's only been ten minutes. Even if she's in bed, I'm sure she's not asleep. Here.'' He put the phone in her hand. "I'll turn on the map light so you can see.''

She only hesitated for a moment, then punched in the digits. At first it was obvious that no one picked up, because Catherine started talking to him. Suddenly it was as if the floodgates had opened. David had a hard time concentrating on his driving because she was pouring her heart out to Shannon.

For a woman who hadn't wanted to know anything about her biological family, she'd done a three-hundred-sixty-degree turn. The more he listened, the more he hoped the love conveyed by her words would work themselves straight into Shannon's heart.

Of the two, Catherine was definitely the more fragile, although *she* believed it was the other way around. As Jack had said earlier, Shannon was the tough one. Looking after herself for the past year had made her more resilient.

When all the words were said, he watched her stare absently out the window, unwilling or unable to make conversation with him.

David decided not to push it. In fact, he didn't speak to her again until he discovered he was hungry and had pulled off at an exit to find a restaurant.

"What would you like to eat?"

"Nothing for me."

He ordered two cheeseburgers with colas anyway. It didn't take him long to devour his before he headed for Portland once more. Not until they got to the city limits did he see her reach for the sack and start eating.

"Why did you take this exit?"

Pleased that she'd noticed, he said, "There's something I want to show you before we go home."

"I'm too tired, David. Morning's going to be here before we know it. I have to be at the office early."

"It's not that far out of our way. Have you been to this area before?"

"No. But everyone in the office has been talking about it since it was developed for residential use."

The destination he had in mind was a ridge overlooking the city, a heavily wooded spot. He eventually drew to a stop so they could look out.

The July night was balmy. With the windows down, he could hear the crickets and smell the fresh, piney scent of the trees.

"What do you think?"

She gazed in rapt attention. "It's a magnificent view."

"I think so, too. Twelve acres have been designated for every lot."

"Whoever owns this piece of property is a very lucky person."

He took a deep breath. "It's yours."

Her head jerked around. "What did you say?"

At last he'd pulled her out of the semitrance she'd been in. "I bought it for you as a wedding present. I had my attorney put it in your name. The first time I came up here, I could envision us living here. I could imagine our children—"

"No!"

She quickly averted her eyes. "You shouldn't have told me that. We shouldn't have come up here. I can't marry you, David. It's my fault that we're together at all tonight.

"Shannon didn't want to be found. I made a grave error in judgment. Please take me back to your place so I can get my car and go home."

With her request spoken in that tremulous voice, he had no choice but to do her bidding. At least he had the satisfaction of knowing he'd been able to show her something she wouldn't be able to put out of her mind. That was the whole idea.

When they reached her car, he insisted that he'd follow her home.

"Don't tell me not to see you to your door," he

said. "I don't care how much security your building has, this late at night it's dangerous. Any place is."

Once they arrived at her building, he walked her to the door. Before she could unlock it and enter, he caught her by the shoulders and gave her a long, hard kiss on the mouth.

"I'll phone you tomorrow," he said as he walked away.

She was on the verge of calling him back—simply because of the desire he'd aroused with that one kiss. Instead, she hurried to her bedroom and got ready for bed. But she might as well not have bothered, because she couldn't sleep. Too much had happened.

She replayed every moment until her mind was spinning. At her wit's end, she got up and worked at her drafting table until dawn crept into the room. Then she took a shower and went to work.

It was seven-thirty when she let herself into the office—late enough that she felt she could call Jack without waking him.

"CC? Long time, no see. What's got you up with the birds this morning?"

"Something awful happened yesterday." Without preamble, she described the sequence of events that had brought her world crashing down around her. By the time she'd finished, she was in tears. "If Shannon comes back to the condo today, she probably won't stay any longer than it takes to pack her clothes. I can't go over to talk to her. I'm in the middle of a huge project—I'm due out at a new site and I'll be spending the whole day there.

"Do you think you could drive to my place and wait for her? I'd hate for her to come home to an empty house. I know it's a lot to ask, Jack. Maybe Melanie could get the day off so she could be with you?"

Jack hadn't answered yet; Catherine took a deep breath and forged on. "If you can't, then I'll ask Mom. I'm sure she would go if I tell her why. It's just that Shannon feels comfortable with you and might confide in you more readily than she would in—"

"Hey, I'll do it," he broke in.

"Thank you. There's one more thing—"

"I know what you're going to say. I'll tell her she has a home with Mom and Dad anytime she wants."

She sniffed. "Thank you, Jack."

"What about David?"

"What about him?"

There was a harsh intake of breath. "Forget I asked."

JACK MADE HIMSELF at home in front of Catherine's TV. Melanie would be over at noon with some lunch. In the meantime, he'd brought a stack of racing videos he needed to review.

He didn't have an answering machine in his apartment. CC's drove him crazy. Every time the phone rang, he ignored it, then had to pay the price of listening to the messages. He was ready to throw something at it—until he heard Phil's voice. Then he grinned.

"Shannon? This is Phil. I know you couldn't have forgotten me already. I'm giving notice that this is the third time I've called you. Three strikes and you're out. You have my number. This is your last opportunity."

Still chuckling, Jack slid in the first tape and sat cross-legged on the floor, his nose practically to the screen. He'd barely started to watch when he heard the static noise that meant there was another call and the machine was going on again.

"Catherine? I'm calling to let you know that I have to go out of town. My mother's brother-in-law died last night. I didn't hear about it until this morning when she phoned me. The family is flying to Detroit this afternoon. There won't be a funeral. Just graveside services. I expect we'll be gone three days. I'll call you this evening to find out if there's been any news about Shannon. I love you. Never forget that."

When he heard David's voice shake, Jack swallowed hard.

Good grief, CC. How long are you going to keep this up?

He settled down once more and managed to watch a half hour's worth of tape before another voice carried into the room.

"Hello, Shannon. You know who this is. Just in case it makes a difference, I'm calling to tell you that I turn twenty-five tomorrow. How about celebrating with me?''

Jack turned down the volume and sat up. Who the hell was this guy? His voice sounded familiar, but Jack couldn't place him.

''All you have to do is call the steakhouse and leave a message. I'll get it.''

The steakhouse. It was Steve, the waiter! *Well, what do you know?* Jack smiled and turned up the volume. Another hour went by before he heard a different sound.

Someone was trying to get in. He got to his feet as Shannon opened the door. Catherine's instincts had been right.

''Jack!'' Shannon cried as she walked in. ''What are you doing here?''

''I've been waiting for you.''

She shut the door. ''Where's Catherine?''

''CC had to go out to a new site today. She's been worried sick about you and asked me to house-sit until you got home.''

Shannon had the grace to look sheepish. ''I was so upset I went back to Tacoma.''

''That's what I figured.'' He moved closer to her. ''Do you hate me, too, for not being up-front with you from the very beginning?''

''I did,'' she murmured.

''Whew… I'm glad you put that in the past tense because I want to make you a proposition.''

''What's that?''

"You and CC need some space. Come out to the house and stay with us for a while."

She shook her head. "I couldn't do that to your family."

"Shannon, Mom and Dad told me to ask you." He paused. "There's something else I need to tell you."

Her head was still bowed. "What?"

"They're really upset that you and CC were separated at birth. They meant what they said—they would have adopted both of you girls had they known the situation.

"Right now, they're ready to love you as their own daughter. They know you had a wonderful family, but they'd like to be your second family if you'd *let* them.

"I'd like you to live at the house, but my reasons are a lot more selfish. When CC moved out, she left a big void. Having you around would fill it again.

"The crew thinks you're cool. They want you to hang out with them, too, especially Phil. He told me he asked you to dinner, but you haven't even called him back to say no. This morning he left another message for you."

"He did?"

"Yeah. You can listen to it yourself. He puts on a tough front, but I think he's pretty crushed.

"You know, he was never interested in CC romantically. He liked teasing her, but he's not laughing about this. So, if you don't have any feelings for him, at least be gentle. He's my buddy."

Without waiting for an invitation, Jack closed the distance and threw an arm around her shoulder. She was crying. "Please come home with us. Please?"

She made a choking sound, then gave a short laugh. "You're impossible to stay mad at, Jack."

"That's what Melanie tells me."

After a pause, she asked, "Your parents really want me there?" The tremor in her voice shot straight to his heart. She sounded just like CC at her most vulnerable.

"Everyone wants you there. CC most of all. She loves you, Shannon—you're her sister. She'd do anything for you."

He felt her ease out of his arms. "I—I don't want her to."

"What do you mean?"

"I mean she doesn't have to give up David for me."

CHAPTER FOURTEEN

JACK STARTED TO GET that tingly feeling. It was the same feeling he always got at the track when he was on his last lap and knew he was going to win.

"She already has said goodbye. It's over for them."

He heard her sigh. "Not if I can help it. Jack? Do you know which site she's gone to?"

His adrenaline started to kick in. "No, but you can call her secretary. Janine will give you the address."

"Depending on the outcome of my conversation with her, I'll either move back to Tacoma or accept your invitation for a temporary stay until I can find a permanent place to live here in Portland." Tears trickled down her cheeks as she spoke.

Jack had been prepared to accept Shannon into their lives. He'd liked her from the outset. But it was pure love he was feeling as he pulled her into his arms and gave her a hug.

"You and CC are identical in more ways than the physical. At heart, you're both good, unselfish people who put others first. Welcome to the family."

She started sobbing in earnest.

Jack had a remedy for those tears. He played back

the two messages, and she listened avidly. It didn't take long for her to regain her composure.

"So, Steve's pretty interested in you. I thought as much when you told me he drove all the way to Tacoma to help you out."

To his surprise, she looked embarrassed. "He's too young."

"Doesn't sound like it to me. Some guys are old at twenty. Some men are kids at ninety."

She ran a hand through her hair. The gesture was so reminiscent of Catherine, he was stunned. "If I were to go out with him for his birthday, would you and Melanie come along? I'd like your opinion."

"We'd love it. But there's a condition," he added.

"What?"

"You give Phil equal time. One date. If it doesn't work out, there's no harm done."

"All right." She finally agreed after a long hesitation.

"Call him now. He's at the garage. It'll make his day."

"You mean right this minute?"

"Yeah. Before you get cold feet."

When she came out of her bedroom fifteen minutes later, he saw a faint pink tinge on her cheeks.

"Did you spend all that time talking to Phil, or did you phone Steve, too?"

"I'll call him tonight when he's at work."

"I have a feeling life around the Casey house is

going to get complicated. Tell you what. I'm going to leave so you can do whatever you need to do."

He gathered up his tapes. "Tomorrow I'll get some of the guys to help move your stuff. You can come out to the house anytime. Today if you want. We're ready for you."

Shannon followed him to the door, then gave him a kiss on the cheek. "Thank you for everything," she whispered.

An overjoyed Jack headed immediately for home. When his cell phone rang, he reached for it, never stopping to glance at the caller ID.

"Jack?"

"Hey, David!"

"Any news?" The agony in his voice left nothing to the imagination.

Jack smiled. "Not yet. But it's still early days."

"This isn't any good, Jack. Last night I was with your sister. We drove to Tacoma to see Shannon, but she wouldn't even come to the door of her friend's apartment. It ripped Catherine apart all over again. I can feel her slipping farther and farther away from me."

"You've got to be patient."

"I don't know if I can."

"I know what you mean. But in CC's case, this is going to take a little more time."

"I'm leaving for Detroit today to attend a family funeral. Call me if you know anything. I don't care if it's the middle of the night. I should be home in three days."

"I will. You call me, too. Anytime. We'll get together as soon as you get back."

CATHERINE WALKED Dean Kooning to the door of the trailer and said good-night. After spending hours going over the blueprints with the acting foreman on the new project, she was exhausted.

Her lack of sleep had taken its toll. She felt numb, barely able to function. Until Sol got out of the hospital, it looked like she'd have to spend the next week at the site making sure everything went according to her specifications.

She sat in the chair, trying to summon the energy to gather up her things and leave. She closed her eyes, too physically and emotionally drained to move. When Shannon entered the trailer, Catherine thought she must be dreaming.

"Is it really you?" she whispered in disbelief.

"Yes. Mind if I come in?"

Catherine felt a surge of excitement. She wanted to throw her arms around her sister, but she didn't know what kind of a reception she'd get, so she stayed where she was.

"Please. Sit down."

"Thanks. After the way I treated you last night, I'm surprised you're still speaking to me."

"It was wrong of us to intrude. Last night was a mistake from start to finish."

"Not yours, Catherine. Mine," Shannon muttered. "But I was in a bad way and didn't want you to see how upset I was. I looked absolutely awful."

"You couldn't possibly have looked as bad as I know I look right now."

"I didn't sleep a wink."

"Neither did I."

"You're sure you don't mind my coming to the site?"

"Of course not! In fact, I'm thrilled."

Catherine was so glad, so relieved that nothing terrible had happened to her sister, she felt light-headed.

"I'm sorry if I worried you."

"You had every right to run off after being betrayed by people you should have had every reason to trust. I'm the one who's sorry—for everything. I never meant to hurt you."

"I know you didn't. The truth is, I didn't mean to say such harsh things and then alarm you by disappearing. But I had to be by myself to...to get my head on straight."

"I understand. Yesterday was the most ghastly day I've ever experienced. I can't even *begin* to imagine your state of mind."

"I admit yesterday was a day I wouldn't care to repeat. But after thinking everything over, I can tell you there's one thing you could do that would take away my pain."

Grasping for anything to improve the situation, Catherine lifted her head. "What is it?" she asked eagerly. "You know if it's humanly possible I'll do it."

Shannon stared straight at her. "You promise?"

"Yes," she answered in a solemn voice.

"You swear before God?"

"I swear it."

"Go to David and make up with him."

"No!" Catherine cried in anger and sprang to her feet. "That's the one thing I won't do!"

"But you promised!"

"I thought— I didn't know this was going to be about David. I wouldn't dream of getting back together with him. What he said after we'd already broken up was needless and unutterably cruel. It caused you untold pain.

"Do you honestly believe I could ever enjoy being with him again knowing how much it would hurt you? You're my *sister*. I love you. You're always going to be in my life. I want us to start fresh. A new beginning. No history."

Shannon shook her head. "That works fine in a fairy tale. But as a wise person recently told me, it's pure fiction. We're two grown women who need to deal with reality."

"David's out of my life."

"Let me ask you a question, Catherine. Do you really want me in yours?"

"More than anything in the world!"

"If that's the truth, then I want you and David to get back together. Otherwise I can't stay in Portland knowing I'm the reason you broke your engagement." She took a deep, shuddering breath.

"Catherine, listen to me," she went on. "Do you have any idea how it would make me feel to live around you day after day, aware that my presence prevented you from being with the man you love? Do you know what a nightmare that would be? How absurd? Talk about cruel!''

Catherine couldn't take it in. ''But…but you met David first and you fell in love—''

''No!'' Shannon blurted. ''I had a long talk with Amy last night. She shared some insights with me from this book she bought—it's a woman's guide to marriage, and it's the first book that's ever changed my life. Anyway, Amy helped me realize what I've always known deep down but never wanted to admit to myself.

''What I felt for David wasn't love. It was infatuation. I've been infatuated with other men before, and I suppose I will be again. The point is, that's all it was.

''David was attracted to me, too, but before the evening was over his attraction wore off. My pride couldn't take it, so I lived in a state of denial hoping he would miraculously change his mind and come to love me. I was pathetic, you know? I became oversensitive, out of control. Visiting his office, trying to get him to go out with me.

''I even went so far as to apply for a job at his clinic so I could be around him. I'm not proud of the fact that I let you believe I applied for the nursing position at Sacred Heart Hospital to be near you. That wasn't the case. At least not entirely.

''I also lied when I told you that I broke up with the man I lived with because he didn't want children and I did. In reality, when I moved in with him, he never made any promises. I went into the relationship thinking I could change him. Of course it didn't work.

"I've really messed up where men are concerned, Catherine. After talking to Amy and reading the book from cover to cover, I can see that I've made practically every mistake on the list. Maybe I'll get it right next time. So for starters, I'm going to move out of your condo."

"No, Shannon! You don't have to go anywhere!"

"Yes, I do. You're going to be getting married and you need to feel free to do whatever you want with your condo. Jack's invited me to stay at your parents' home until I can find a permanent place of my own."

Thank you, Jack Casey.

Catherine nodded. "Mom and Dad suggested it last week."

"That's what he said. I can't tell you what it means to know your family wants me around." Her voice trembled.

Catherine was dazed with joy and only half believed this conversation was really taking place. "We all want you around. Forever!"

"If that's true," Shannon said, getting to her feet to take hold of Catherine's hands, "promise me you'll marry David as you planned. Then I can be happy in my new life. Will you do that for me?"

"Shannon…" She caught her sister to her heart. They clung for a long time.

"Enough of this." Shannon sniffed hard before they finally released each other. "You need to find David right away, and I need to call Steve."

"The waiter?"

She grinned. "Yes. He's been trying to get me to go out with him. In fact, he called this morning and left a message on your machine. Jack convinced me to say yes. He said he and Melanie would join us. I'm not a very good judge of character when it comes to men, but I have a feeling Jack will be able to size him up in a hurry."

"He sure will, and he'll be blunt about it, too!" They both laughed.

"What about Phil?"

"I've agreed to go out with him, as well. I've learned that I need to be open to all kinds of possibilities—dredge all kinds of ponds."

Catherine didn't understand that remark but let it go. "Well, I can tell you one thing about Phil. He'd never call a woman unless he meant it. I'm jealous to think he's already phoned you twice."

"Actually, he phoned this morning, too. I guess I'm going to find out how interested he really is. I called him at the garage. We have a date for brunch next Sunday at the Sky Castle."

"That's wonderful news," Catherine said softly. "But the best news is, I have a sister. I always wanted one."

"So did I."

"We've got years and years to be together." Catherine couldn't stop smiling.

"We'll grow old together."

"We'll always have each other."

"What if my mother had never told me I had a twin?"

"But she did. Our lives are richer because of it."

"Yes."

"I love you, Shannon."

"And I love you. Now let's get you out of here because there's a man waiting to hear from you. I think it's time you put him out of his agony."

As THE PLANE began its descent to the Portland airport, David felt despair overwhelm him. Catherine was somewhere in that city, but she wouldn't be waiting for him.

On this short trip, which had resulted in his aunt Colleen's coming to stay with his mother for a while, David had begun to think that living in Portland was no longer good for him.

"Are you sure you don't want company?" Mitch asked an hour later, after they'd settled their mother and aunt at the house.

"You know something, Mitch? You've had to put up with my foul mood long enough. Thanks for being there. Now I think I'd better spend some time alone. Open the trunk, will you?"

He levered himself from the passenger seat of Mitch's car to retrieve his suitcase.

"David?" his brother called. "Remember, Jack told you not to give up hope."

"When Catherine threw my wedding present

back in my face, Jack wasn't there to hear her tell me she couldn't marry me. I've finally come to the conclusion that this dream is truly over.''

Mitch eyed him sorrowfully. ''If it wasn't meant to be, just remember that one day someone else will come along.''

He shrugged. ''I've lived on this earth long enough to know that's true. But she won't be Catherine. What really scares me is that I'll be looking for her in every woman I meet. I'm afraid that when I can't find her, I'll move on, never able to settle.

''It might not be a bad idea if I left Portland and lived someplace else, someplace completely different. Maybe even out of the country. The thought of being in the same city with her, knowing she's here but never being able to see her, is just too painful.''

''David, you sound too depressed to be alone. Let's go out for a drink.''

''Not a good idea. When I can't stand my own company, I wouldn't dare inflict myself on you.''

''I'd tell you to go home and get drunk, but I know it wouldn't help. Well...I'll call you later to see how you're doing.''

As Mitch drove away, David was already entertaining the idea of making Dr. Kamura acting head of the institute. The move would free David to go anywhere in the world. Russia needed outside business to help bring money to its struggling economy. Maybe he could set up a day trading company there.

The administrative challenges involved, not to mention the language difficulties in getting established, sounded like exactly the kind of consuming distraction he needed.

He nodded to some acquaintances who lived in his building, then rode the elevator to the fifth floor. Frustrated because it was too late in the day to find out if his idea of setting up a business in Russia was feasible, he entered his apartment in the blackest of moods, tossing his suitcase carelessly aside.

Mitch's suggestion about getting drunk propelled him to the kitchen, where he knew there was a bottle of Scotch on the shelf. But before he could reach for it, he saw something propped on the counter. Some sort of painting or poster.

It brought him to an abrupt halt. He glanced around, puzzled. It meant he'd had a visitor at his condo while he'd been gone.

As he moved closer to see what it was, the blood started to pound in his ears. With a sense of wonder he took in the breathtaking watercolor—a rendering of an exquisite French country home designed in Catherine Casey's inimitable style.

His gaze shifted to the printing at the bottom.

Residence of Mr. and Mrs. David M. Britton.

The words filled his vision before they echoed in his heart.

"Catherine?"

He heard a footfall behind him and wheeled, out of breath. There stood the woman he loved. She was in T-shirt and jeans, wearing a hard hat. She smiled at him, the way she had that day at the speedway.

Her gray eyes virtually blinded him with their radiance.

"Mr. Britton? I thought you'd never get here. I'm Catherine Casey. I know you were expecting Cameron Casey, but I told him this project was mine, because I'm in love with the client. You see, I know his soul. I know his wants and needs better than anyone else alive because I have those same wants and needs." She swallowed. "In fact, I still have the designs for his office complex on my computer at work. Any time he's interested in starting that project, I'm ready. Mr. Casey approves."

"Darling—"

"I also informed Mr. Casey that you and I are getting married on September first. Lucky for me, he approves of that, too. He kindly relieved me of all other responsibilities so I could get started on this lifetime project immediately.

"As soon as your friend Allen learned why I needed to get into your condo, he couldn't have been more accommodating. I'm pretty sure your mom and mine will be on the phone shortly to plan our wedding. They'll have a lot of extra help now that Shannon's moved to the house.

"If I don't miss my guess, the folks have already installed her in my old bedroom. I hear she's getting along really well with the crew. I'd be jealous if I wasn't so deeply in love with the most wonderful man I've ever met.

"David, how can I ever thank you for going

ahead and telling Shannon the truth? She sought Amy's help, and that turned everything around.

"She begged me to get back together with you. I knew she meant it with all her heart. In that moment, we became close the way twin sisters should be. The past is behind us.

"Your instincts were right all along. Hiding our love from her was the worst thing I could have done. Everyone's suffered because of my fears.

"Please forgive me, David. I'll never knowingly hurt you again. I love you. I want to be your wife as soon as you'll have me."

Never underestimate the power of your love.

After the long period of darkness, the sunlight was too dazzling. David couldn't seem to function in his dazed condition. What he needed was to find comfort in Catherine's arms. Then he'd know this was real.

As he reached for her, the hard hat fell to the floor, but neither of them noticed or cared.

October 8

WHILE CATHERINE STOOD in the kitchen drinking some milk to settle her stomach, she heard a key in the lock. The next thing she knew, her brother waltzed through the door.

"Jack!" she squealed in delight. Setting her glass on the counter, she rushed toward him, almost stumbling over the bags she had yet to unpack from their honeymoon. She and David had decided to stay in her condo until their house was built.

Her brother caught her in his arms and swung her around.

"Welcome home, CC! After five weeks, I thought maybe you and David had decided to set up residence in Greece."

"We were tempted, believe me. Corfu is so fabulous you'll have to go there on your honeymoon. How soon's your wedding?"

"Two weeks away."

"Melanie must be ecstatic."

"Yeah." Jack studied her. "Marriage looks good on you, CC. I can tell my brother-in-law has made you very happy."

"You can't even imagine," she whispered emotionally.

"I think I can. You're pregnant, aren't you?"

"*Jack!*" She blushed. "How could you know something like that?"

"Just a guess." He shrugged expansively. "I know it's a cliché, but there's a glow about you."

She shook her head in amazement. "A few minutes ago, I did a home pregnancy test. It came out positive! Can you believe it?" she cried. "I'm going to be a mother! David has no idea that in about eight months he's going to be a father. He'll be so thrilled. I can't wait to tell him!"

"No one deserves good news more than he does." A seriousness had crept into Jack's voice.

"I'm so thankful you and David are friends."

"Your husband's incredible, CC. While you were on your honeymoon, an anonymous donor put funds in my bank account. It was enough money for me to start building a formula one car.

"Dad swore he didn't do it. I don't know anyone else with that kind of cash who'd be willing to back me. David didn't tell you?"

Catherine's heart rate had gone off the charts. "No. But I know he was the one who did it. In Corfu he confided what a wonderful friend you were to him through our crisis. He said that when the going got really rough, you encouraged him and gave him hope. You took time off work to help him clarify his feelings. That's what he said—and that he owed you big time."

Jack grinned. "I got paid big time. But with or without the money, I have to tell you he's the perfect man for you, CC."

"I agree. And you've always been the perfect brother. How's my twin doing?"

"She's decided Steve's not the guy for her, but they're still pretty friendly. I like him, too. Now Phil, on the other hand... That's getting serious. He's acting like a man on the verge of you know what."

"Honestly?"

"Would I lie to you? The sparks are flying. Ask any of the crew."

"You have no idea how happy I am to hear that."

"Sure I do."

She laughed out loud. "Of course you do. You know me better than I know myself."

"Which means I know I should get out of here so you can go see your husband and tell him the good news."

"That's exactly what I'm going to do!"

"Come by the house tomorrow. Everyone'll want to hear there's going to be a new addition to the family. Later on, if you find out it's a boy, I won't mind if you name him Jack."

Her eyes filled with tears. "I already gave that some thought."

"Love you." He kissed her cheek before she walked him to the door.

"Oh—before I forget. The attorney who handled your adoption found the record of your birth in Tacoma, Washington. Your birth mother had twins at a private clinic. It took a subpoena to get into their files, which is the reason Shannon couldn't come up with any information.

"He found out that your birth father was not her husband. She gave up one of her babies for adoption in Tacoma, then moved to Portland and eventually gave you up.

"There's no record of her living in Portland after your adoption. Somehow she had the documents falsified for the agency used by Mom and Dad's attorney. That's why you didn't know you were a twin. It explains why Shannon's mother knew about the other twin."

Catherine nodded. "According to Shannon, her

adoptive father didn't want another child. If he'd been willing, I would have ended up living in Tacoma with Shannon.''

''Well I'm glad you ended up being my sister.''

Their eyes were suspiciously bright as they smiled at each other.

''Dad's attorney is still trying to track down your birth mother, but he thinks it could take a long time. Maybe he'll never be able to find her. It's his opinion that since your birth mother decided you two would be better off with adoptive parents, she probably didn't want to be found. But it's up to you and Shannon if you'd like the attorney to keep searching.''

''I don't want that, but Shannon might feel differently.''

''I don't know. She loves Mom and Dad like her own already.''

''Was there ever any doubt?''

''Nope.''

''But you're going to keep looking for your birth parents, right?''

''Wrong.''

Catherine was so shocked, her mouth fell open. Speechless, she stared at him.

Jack smiled slightly at her reaction. ''After what we've all lived through, I've changed my mind. In fact, I've decided I'm going to concentrate on being a good husband, like David. He's my new role model. Know what I mean? See you later.''

She hugged herself in happiness as he walked out

the door, then rushed to get ready to see her husband. David had been gone from his office so long, one more day of interruption wasn't going to make any difference. Not considering the news she had to tell him.

After slipping a set of the blueprints for their house in a portfolio, she left for his office, breathless with excitement.

"Good morning, Louise."

The older woman eyed her uncertainly.

Catherine decided to take compassion on her. "I'm David's wife."

"Oh!"

"Don't worry about it. People confuse me and Shannon all the time."

"Welcome home, Mrs. Britton! Congratulations. Your wedding was so beautiful, I felt honored to be invited."

"We were pleased you could come. Is my husband alone?"

"Yes, but not for long. He's called a staff meeting. It's supposed to start in twenty minutes."

"In that case, I'd better hurry."

Her heart pounding, she opened the door of his office. He was on the phone, but the second he caught sight of her, he said goodbye to whoever it was and shot out of his seat.

"Catherine! How did you know I was wishing you were here!"

He drew her into his arms and kissed her, then kissed her again. Their hunger knew no limits. She moaned with desire. All he had to do was look at her, touch her, and her body went up in flames.

Those days and nights in Corfu had been a time of endless pleasure. They'd explored and worshiped each other's bodies until she'd felt she was a living, breathing part of him. This morning when they'd awakened, he hadn't wanted to get out of bed, and she'd done everything in her power to keep him there.

"I'm on the way to my office, but I thought I'd better stop by here first to consult with you on a change to our house plans."

"Whatever you want is fine with me. You know that," he murmured, kissing her cheeks and throat, holding her body tight against his.

Gasping for breath, she wriggled free of his grasp and picked up the portfolio, which had fallen to the floor. "I think this is something that should have your input."

With trembling hands, she opened the folder and pulled out the blueprints. He cleared his desk so she could set them down.

"What would you think if we made another room off the master bedroom?"

He stared at the design, not comprehending. "But we already have four bedrooms."

"Yes, I know. This would be a little room."

"You mean like an extra closet?"

"Not exactly. It would have to have a window to let in the light."

The puzzlement on his handsome face was comical. "What would we use it for?"

The happiness suddenly faded from his eyes. "You're thinking of sleeping in there without me?"

"Maybe. Sometimes. Or possibly the other way around."

His look grew fierce. "I got married to sleep with my wife. Every night of my life!"

"Well, you might have to break that vow once in a while."

"Why?" he demanded tersely. "What happened on our honeymoon that's caused you to think this way?"

"Quite a lot happened, actually."

She watched him swallow. "Dammit, Catherine! Tell me what's wrong."

His mouth tautened. Catherine thought that by now he would have caught on. His distress was growing and she realized she'd better give him a more obvious clue. Grabbing one of his felt tip pens, she drew a room off the master bedroom and wrote in the word *nursery*.

He stared at it for a full minute. Then his head reared back. "We're pregnant?"

"Yes, darling."

"Already?"

"Yes! I slipped out after you left this morning and bought one of those home pregnancy kits. The test came out positive!"

"You're sure it's reliable?"

"Even without the test, I suspected I was pregnant. For one thing, I've been nauseated for the last few days.''

He slid his hand to her stomach. "Do you think there might be two babies growing in there?"

"David—! I forgot about that. With twins in your family and in my biological family, it's more than possible."

"Maybe you'd better draw two nurseries in the plans, just in case."

Once again their mouths met in joy and passion.

Ten minutes later David buzzed his secretary. "Louise? Cancel the staff meeting. My wife and I are going home to celebrate the news that I'm going to be a father. Our baby might even turn out to be twins."

"Oh—that's wonderful! Congratulations."

"I think *you're* wonderful, Mr. Britton," Catherine whispered against his mouth. "And so will your children."

HARLEQUIN®
SUPERROMANCE®

*Pregnant and alone—
these stories follow women
from the heartache of
betrayal to finding true love
and starting a family.*

THE FOURTH CHILD by C.J. Carmichael.
When Claire's marriage is in trouble, she tries to
save it—although she's not sure she can forgive her
husband's betrayal.
On sale May 2000.

AND BABY MAKES SIX by Linda Markowiak.
Jenny suddenly finds herself jobless and pregnant by
a man who doesn't want their child.
On sale June 2000.

MOM'S THE WORD by Roz Denny Fox.
After her feckless husband steals her inheritance and
leaves town with another woman, Hayley discovers she's
pregnant.
On sale July 2000.

Available wherever Harlequin books are sold.

HARLEQUIN®
Makes any time special ™

WELCOME TO

Crystal Creek

If this is your first visit to the
friendly ranching town in the hill
country of Texas, get ready to meet
some unforgettable people. If you've
been there before, you'll be happy to
see some old faces and meet new ones.

Harlequin Superromance® and Margot Dalton—
author of seven books in the original
Crystal Creek series—are pleased to offer
three **brand-new** stories set in Crystal Creek.

IN PLAIN SIGHT by **Margot Dalton**
On sale May 2000

CONSEQUENCES by **Margot Dalton**
On sale July 2000

THE NEWCOMER by **Margot Dalton**
On sale September 2000

HARLEQUIN®
Makes any time special ™